MASSACRE
AT SAN PABLO

D1453944

**Center Point
Large Print**

**This Large Print Book carries the
Seal of Approval of N.A.V.H.**

MASSACRE
AT SAN PABLO

LEWIS B. PATTEN

CENTER POINT PUBLISHING
THORNDIKE, MAINE

This Center Point Large Print edition
is published in the year 2008 by arrangement with
Golden West Literary Agency.

The text of this Large Print edition is unabridged. In other
aspects, this book may vary from the original edition.
Printed in the United States of America.
Set in 16-point Times New Roman type.

ISBN: 978-1-60285-176-4

Library of Congress Cataloging-in-Publication Data

Patten, Lewis B.
    Massacre at San Pablo / Lewis B. Patten.--Center Point large print ed.
        p. cm.
    ISBN 978-1-60285-176-4 (lib. bdg. : alk. paper)
    1. Large type books. I. Title.

PS3566.A79M368 2008
813'.54--dc22

2007051299

Chapter 1

AT THE END of day, the desert lay flat and shimmering behind them and they began the long climb toward the high-piled, rocky mountains ahead.

The brilliant hues of the setting sun dyed the thin clouds gold and rose, yet of all the passengers in the stagecoach, only one noticed the radiant beauty in the sky.

Mark Atkins, a boy of twelve, sat by the window, his shoulder bracing his body against the swaying of the coach, against its jolting rattle, and stared at the land, at the sky, at the towering saguaros.

His face showed weariness, but his eyes were bright with an interest that hadn't flagged once during the long monotony of the journey. In the fading light, the saguaros became giants, their arms upraised, or soldiers marching in column across the dusty desert floor. A bobcat was briefly visible as she walked disdainfully from rock to rock; he saw the coyote, later, that spooked up from the noise of the coach and slunk quickly into a dry arroyo.

His father woke from a restless sleep, mopped his face with a soiled bandanna and said to no one in particular, "Beats me how that boy can sit there day after day and stare at this damned desert."

Mark turned and smiled at his father, and the man tousled his hair affectionately. His mother, her face gaunt and shining with perspiration, smiled at the two with weary fondness. They were bound for Los Angeles, and she had had no sleep for the past three nights. But Tucson was ahead, and they'd rest in Tucson for two or three days. After that, the remainder of the journey would be bearable.

The rose-gold clouds faded slowly to purple and gray. Mark's mother put her head against her husband's shoulder. The boy stared out at the darkening landscape, absorbed and entranced by the way it changed in the fading light.

The coach's jolting increased, for here the road was rocky and much rougher than it had been before. The boy braced himself more firmly and his mother uttered a low, protesting groan.

A shrill cry, alien and strange, made the boy's eyes lift to the slope above. He saw dust boiling up from the hoofs of a dozen sliding, plunging ponies. And Mark had his first glimpse of Apaches in the uncertain light of dusk, clinging like cockleburrs to the backs of those sliding ponies.

Now their cries lifted like shrill coyote barks in the still, hot air. The shotgun of the guard up on the box roared once, twice. The driver's long whip cracked savagely, and the teams lunged against their collars and broke into a hard run.

The Indians slid into the road behind the coach and galloped after it, firing bows and guns.

Mark's father yanked him away from the window and shoved him and his mother down onto the floor of the coach. Mark was jammed hard against the door when the other passenger, a fat little man in a crumpled business suit, joined them on the floor.

Mark's father poked his head and right arm out the window and began to fire methodically with his old percussion pistol at the howling savages behind the coach. The guard's shotgun roared again and again.

Mark's mother began to cry almost soundlessly, as much from exhaustion as from fear, and the fat passenger on the floor with them began to pray incoherently.

The coach lurched around a sharp turn, swaying dangerously. Behind it, the Apache guns barked vengefully.

Then all was confusion and shattering chaos. An Apache bullet had taken one of the horses in the lead team straight through the neck. The horse dropped.

The following horses piled into the downed horse, kicking, tangling their harness and fighting to be free. The coach slammed into the tangled mass of horses. It tipped, and skidded sideways. A wheel went off the edge, and the coach tilted off the road with an almost deliberate ponderousness.

It rolled twice, pulling the horses off the road in a screaming tangle, then came to rest with a thunderous crash against the trunk of an ancient piñon pine. Baggage and bleeding horses marked its path from the road. Its yellow wheels spun crazily; dust rolled over it in choking clouds. The Apaches swarmed toward the coach, screeching with hate-crazed excitement.

Mark was conscious, first, of flying wildly through

empty air. He seemed to be falling forever. Then he felt his body strike the yielding, prickly branches of a giant cedar, and still he fell. The branches clawed at his clothes and face. His head struck something hard and solid.

Pain roared briefly through him. Then he knew no more.

The sun was rising over the desert when Mark came to. He began to cry at once, from pain and shock, but then memory came washing over him and he remembered the Indians. His crying stopped immediately and for a moment he held his breath in fright.

He was wedged in the crotch of an enormous cedar tree. Sharp pains ran through his right leg. His head ached terribly.

He moved, and a gasping groan escaped his lips. He righted himself in the crotch of the tree and slipped to the ground, only three or four feet below him.

The slope here was steep. His right leg went out from under him and he fell. He rolled eight feet down the slope before he could stop.

He lay still, arms and legs outspread, the side of his face against the cool, shaly slope. He whimpered softly a few moments, pain and exhaustion washing through his body.

Gradually his whimpering ceased, but still he did not move. Listening intently, he heard the chatter of a magpie, and nothing else.

He pulled his legs under him and got up slowly.

He was tall for his age, his frame slender from rapid growth. His baggy wool trousers were torn and he stopped to brush at them ineffectually.

He straightened, then, and lifted a skinned hand to brush at his shock of yellow hair. The expression in his eyes and on his face betrayed a fearful unconscious knowledge—he was alone in the middle of the Arizona desert; all the others. . . .

He should have heard some sound! He *had* to hear some sound!

Frantically now, caring not for the noise he made, he scrambled up the slope, stumbling, sliding, clawing and pumping with hands and feet.

He stopped and lay flat on the slope, panting. There was a smell in the air now, one no man can describe—the smell of blood and death.

A primeval dread stirred the hair on the back of Mark's neck, overcame him, settling like a dark blanket over his mind.

The sun sifting through the cedars, was warm on his back. The air was dry and clear. Glancing back out across the desert, he could see clearly for a hundred miles, and in all that monstrous waste nothing stirred or moved.

He rose to his knees again. His eyes were wide, his mouth compressed. His nostrils flared. One of his cheekbones, noticeably high even in a childishly rounded face, was skinned and scabbed.

He labored up the slope and saw the coach at last, lying on its side. Beyond it he saw the baggage strewn about. The bags had been cut open with knives, and apparel of all kinds lay scattered on the ground.

A horse lay on its back, four feet pointing at the sky. Its throat had been cut and a black streak of dried blood flowed from its neck and down the slope.

Mark began to run. The smell was stronger now, but so still was the air that the violence which had spawned this ene seemed far away. All Mark had to do was find his father and mother. They would know what to do next.

He saw his mother first. She lay face down as though she had been running and had tripped and fallen.

Tears of relief came to Mark's eyes. With a sob that caught in his throat, he stumbled to her and fell on his knees beside her. He buried his face against her.

But there was no warmth in her, no stir of life. Still with his face buried in her clothing, he stiffened and began to turn cold. Slowly, slowly, he pulled his face away and raised his eyes.

Suddenly he was sobbing hysterically. With half-mad strength, he seized her shoulder and rolled her over onto her back.

Her face was strange. She did not even look like his mother. Then his face contorted and a long shudder shook him. Where the hair on the top of her head had been, now there was only dried and blackened blood.

Whiteness began around his mouth and spread slowly until it encompassed his whole face. He closed his eyes and squeezed them more tightly shut.

He got up and stumbled away until he fell. Even then he did not open his eyes. His body was shivering as though he had a chill.

The sun crawled higher in the sky. Vultures circled overhead, gathering from all points of the compass. They too had been drawn by the smell of blood and death. They dropped lower, circling lazily.

Mark Atkins stirred, and their wings beat hard and fast as they lifted warily away. He got up and looked skyward. The shivering became more violent.

His mind pushed away the knowledge of what had happened to his mother. It settled with fixed intensity upon his father. If he could only find his father. . . .

He glanced dazedly around at the macabre scene of destruction. There were other dead horses close by. And over there . . .

But it was the fat man who had cowered on the floor with Mark and his mother. The fat man hadn't been scalped. He was completely bald, and his head glistened whitely in the sun.

Mark found the driver and the shotgun guard lying no more than ten feet apart. Though his stomach was empty, he could feel it churning. He began to sweat, and his face turned gray. He sat down abruptly on a rock and retched, a dry gagging that left him weak and shaking. He got up and wandered on. At last he found his father lying close beside the coach.

He looked and turned away. And now, now that his eyes had verified what his mind already had known, the full impact of a terrible aloneness struck him. He climbed to the road and began to run.

He ran until exhaustion claimed him. Though his mind was almost numb with shock, he knew he could not make it, alone and without water or food, back to the place where the coach had stopped yesterday in late afternoon. And yet, he couldn't return to the wrecked coach, to the broken and mutilated bodies lying scattered about, to the settling vultures and the bloating horses.

The sun beat against his head with merciless intensity. His face, which had been gray with pallor before, was now red from heat.

He found himself some shade under a gnarled cedar above the road. He was thirsty. His right leg, which had been wrenched by his fall, ached dully. Sick and without hope, he buried his face in his arms and began to cry.

In some way, the tears relaxed him. He curled up on the dry, shaly ground. An instant later he was sound asleep, a small and lonely figure, his freckled face streaked with tears and dust.

He could not have slept much more than an hour. And yet, even this short sleep had rested his shocked mind, his exhausted body. When he woke, it was to immediate realization of his predicament, and also to a firmly stubborn sense of responsibility. He began to walk purposefully back up the road toward the wrecked coach.

Two of the vultures were sitting, ghoulish and horrible, on the belly of one of the dead horses. Around the same horse, several more moved awkwardly. Their heads were ugly red, their bodies an unpleasant shade of brown.

Mark stooped and seized a couple of rocks. He flung the rocks at the birds and they rose into the air with a thunderous flapping, and resumed their circling.

For the first time, anger touched him. His gray eyes glittered with it. He searched among the scattered valises until he found a shovel he had seen earlier, one the driver had carried in the luggage boot. It was rusty, but its ash handle was sound.

A light breeze sprang up, blowing toward the shimmering desert floor from the high mountains. The stench of the dead horse came strongly to Mark's nostrils. He hurried off to one side and began to dig in the shade of a gnarled and monstrous piñon pine.

He dug steadily for an hour, but had little to show for his work at the end of that time. He struck crumbled shale six inches under the surface, and it had to be chipped at instead of dug.

He spit on his palms, as he had seen his father do, and went on. Blisters formed on his hands, and broke to become raw sores.

He moved as though in a trance now, his eyes glittering with anger, his mouth drawn into a thin, straight line. He. chipped at the ground with a kind of impersonal animosity.

Slowly the day wore on and slowly the grave became deeper. At a foot and a half, the shale gave way to a sandy loam that was dry as powder. He went on with his task more easily.

His mouth became dry as cotton. His tongue swelled until it seemed to fill his mouth, until he thought it would choke him. His lips cracked and began to bleed. But his anger did not diminish.

In midafternoon he collapsed, though he did not lose consciousness. He thought of water, in the quantity in which he had known it back home—a glassy-surfaced lake, a stream rippling over worn and rounded stones. And suddenly he remembered that there had been water in the coach; his father had had a canteen. So had the fat man. So had the driver and guard.

He got up and staggered toward the wrecked coach. He found a canvas-enclosed canteen lying beside it and wondered why he hadn't noticed it before. He unscrewed the top and drank his fill of the tepid water, and promptly thereafter vomited the water out onto the ground.

Carrying the empty canteen, he went stubbornly back to his work.

The vultures returned, and this time would not be driven away. Mark tried to drag his father's body to the grave, but he was not able to move it more than a few inches.

He sat down. He had reached the limit of his strength. Now there was nothing left to do but wait. Death would find him soon.

Chapter 2

A MILE from the foot of the slope on which the coach had been wrecked, Jaime Ortega and his small family rested in the bottom of an arroyo. The enormous shimmering desert, which to Mark Atkins had appeared so empty, was in reality not empty at all. There was life on the desert, life of all kinds. But in daylight, most living things took cover both from the blazing sun and from their natural enemies.

With Ortega was his wife Rosa María and the nine-year-old son of his sister Lupe Valdez, who had died more than a month before. The boy's name was León. With Ortega too was the small, durable burro upon which rode their food and water, blankets and other necessities. Upon the burro rode also Rosa María, when she was tired, or León.

Mostly, however, they walked. Traveling at night, they had crossed this desert two weeks before, going north to Los Santos to get the orphaned boy. Returning now, they again traveled at night and rested by day, not only to avoid marauding Apaches, but also to spare themselves the merciless heat of the sun.

Jaime Ortega had watched with empty eyes the buzzards gather this morning. He was used to seeing death on the desert. Nor had his concern been roused by the buzzards' failure to alight immediately. Whatever had drawn them still lived, then, but soon would die.

He slept, and roused, and slept again. The heat of day increased. In one of his waking moments, he saw the buzzards drop lower into the cedars that covered the slope. He saw them rise again, flapping their wings as though something had frightened them.

For the first time, Jaime Ortega's brow wrinkled with puzzlement. He glanced at his wife, who was sleeping soundly, and at León near beside her. He got up silently and climbed to the rim of the arroyo. Without showing more than his head, he studied the desert and the mountain slopes with minute care.

Carefully, then, he dropped back into the arroyo and went to Rosa María's side. He touched her shoulder gently, and when she opened her eyes, he said in whispered Spanish, "There is something strange on the mountain slope that I must investigate. Do not be afraid, for there is no danger."

Taking his ancient flintlock musket, he left her and climbed out of the arroyo. Looking back, he saw fear and concern in her dark, liquid eyes. He smiled reassuringly, teeth flashing whitely against his dark skin.

He traveled slowly and with much care, his eyes alert to each small movement within his range of vision.

He was a small, wiry man of thirty-five, whom God had not seen fit to bless with sons. A long mustache adorned his upper lip, and thin black whiskers covered his cheeks and chin. His eyes, deep-set in a sun-darkened, leathery face, were calm and gentle and black as shoe buttons. He wore faded cotton trousers that were ragged at the bottom, straw sandals, a thin cotton shirt, also faded, and a wide-brimmed straw sombrero. A sheathed, razor-sharp knife hung from a thong tied around his waist.

He reached the foot of the slope, noticing that the vultures had alighted again. He shrugged fatalistically, and he almost turned back. He was too late. Whatever had frightened the buzzards no longer frightened them.

He was on a fool's errand anyway, traveling more than a mile in the merciless heat of the sun simply to see buzzards feeding upon a dead animal.

And yet, something within Jaime Ortega kept him from turning back. Something here was not quite right—the actions of the vultures had subtly told him so.

He patiently climbed the slope, making his way through the thick-growing cedars and piñon pine until he reached the site of the wreck.

He halted immediately, his body hidden behind the peeling trunk of a giant cedar.

Many times in his life had he come upon similar scenes, yet in spite of this, shock traveled through him at the thoroughness of the Apaches' barbarity. Then his sweeping glance saw the laboriously dug grave, saw the boy sitting with his head hanging in exhaustion beside the body of a man. He saw the buzzards sitting upon the bloating body of the dead horse, feeding and quarreling as they fed. They rose, flapping noisily, as he stepped out from behind the tree.

Jaime Ortega approached the boy silently, his eyes filled with compassion. He stopped while yet ten feet away and spoke softly in the strongly accented English he had learned from the padre in San Pablo. "Are you hurt, small one?"

Mark Atkins started violently. His eyes, wide with terror, lifted to the dark face before him. He tried to jump up and run, but fell sprawling before he could gain his feet.

Jaime Ortega didn't move, for he could see how near this boy was to the breaking point. Mark's mouth was working violently, but no words came forth.

Jaime said, very softly and very gently, "I have come not to hurt, but to help." He waited, to give the boy's stunned mind time to understand.

Jaime looked at the grave the boy had dug and his eyes brightened with admiration. Sadly he looked at the man on the ground. He said, "This one is your padre?"

Mark nodded dumbly. Some of the terror was fading from his face. Jaime held himself still. "Come, then. I will help you finish the task you have begun so well."

Mark nodded again. He got slowly to his feet. His glance flicked to the body of his mother, and Jaime felt a sudden pity catch at his throat. *"Por Dios!"* he murmured. "Your madre, too?"

Mark nodded. His eyes glistened briefly and his chin quivered. Then his mouth firmed, his face grew still and cold.

Jaime stooped and put his hands under the shoulders of the boy's father. He dragged him laboriously toward the grave, but gently too, wishing he were large enough to lift him.

The boy went and stood beside his mother, but did not look at her.

Jaime returned for her and lifted her in his arms. He carried her to where her husband lay and put her down. Then he went to the wrecked coach and cut away the canvas that had covered the luggage boot. He spread it in the grave and laid the two bodies on it. He folded it over to cover them.

He bent his head and took off his hat. He prayed in Spanish, then for the boy's benefit he said in English, "The Lord giveth and the Lord taketh away. Blessed be the name of the Lord."

Tears streamed silently down the boy's cheeks. Ortega picked up the shovel and filled in the grave. Then he laid it down. "Come with me, *mi hijo.* You cannot remain here. There will be no more coaches passing here for three full days."

The stillness of the boy's face, his expressionless eyes, wrenched at Jaime Ortega's heart. It would be many days before this boy would forget; it would be many, many nights before he would cease to dream and, dreaming, to wake with screams on his lips.

Jaime said, "Come," and walked down the slope in the direction he had come. After a brief hesitation, the boy followed. Behind them, the buzzards alighted again.

Hearing the sound of the boy's steps behind him, Jaime Ortega called back softly, "How are you called, *niño?* What is your name?"

The boy did not answer immediately. At last he said, "Mark. Mark Atkins."

"And you were journeying to Tucson?"

"California."

"You have other relatives? In California, perhaps?"

Mark shook his head.

Jaime said softly, "With me are my wife Rosa María, and my sister's son León. We go to San Pablo, our home, which is fifty miles south of the border. For now you must come with us, but when we reach San Pablo we will talk to the padre and decide what is to be done."

They traveled in silence. When they reached the arroyo, Mark's face was ghastly pale. He tried to climb into the arroyo but fell and rolled to the bottom in a cloud of dust. Ortega jumped down and, touching the boy for the first time, helped him to his feet and dusted him off. Then he led him over to where Rosa María and León were. The boy's hand clung tightly to that of Jaime Ortega.

Jaime said in Spanish, "This is Marcos. The things his eyes have beheld are not things a boy's eyes should see. His mother and father and all those in the stagecoach with them were killed by the Apache last night. God has seen fit to spare the boy and to send me to him. He will go with us and be a brother to León."

Rosa María hurried to get the canteen from the pack. She let Mark have two or three swallows. Then she gave him some pieces of jerky to chew upon. He chewed solemnly, his eyes on her face. When he had finished, she made him lie down.

Perhaps the presence of a woman and another child reassured him. Perhaps Jaime Ortega's kindness had already done so. In any event, Mark Atkins was soon asleep.

For a little while he slept quietly, in complete exhaustion. Then he began to dream. He moaned and jerked in his sleep as his dreaming mind relived the events of the past day, until at last he sat bolt upright on the sandy floor of the arroyo and with his eyes wide open, screaming at the brassy sky.

His body was stiff and cold when Rosa María touched him. He fought when she tried to waken and comfort him. Then it ended at last and he came awake.

His face was rigid with terror, his eyes slow to comprehend that it had been a dream.

Rosa María folded him in her arms and, sitting there on the flat, sandy floor of the arroyo, rocked him in her arms and crooned to him incoherently in Spanish.

The sun was almost down. Jaime Ortega began to repack the burro. He moved leisurely and without haste. The sun had dropped behind the mountains in the west before he had finished.

They ate their supper of cold tortillas and red wine

in the graying light of dusk. Mark was allowed no tortillas, but was given some more jerky and a little wine instead. When they had finished, Jaime climbed out of the arroyo leading the burro. Rosa María herded the two boys before her, and then climbed out last. They headed south in the growing darkness. Mark and León trudged silently behind the burro. Occasionally they would look at each other, shyly and appraisingly.

A numbness was in Mark now, and great weariness. But he moved along without complaint. Anything was better than staying at the site of the wreck. Anything was better than the horror of being alone. He was alone no more, and that was enough for now.

At moonrise, they stopped to rest and eat. León, in addition to being shy, knew no English. Mark knew no Spanish. So they could not talk. But a silent bond grew up between them. Both had been recently orphaned. Both felt strange and lonely.

Neither Jaime nor Rosa María tried to talk to Mark. In their simple, instinctive way, they seemed to know that what he had been through was not something to be forgotten in talk. But they were gentle, and they felt his pain, and this was better for him, perhaps, than all the talk in the world.

They rested briefly, and then went on, traveling steadily until gray began to lighten the eastern horizon.

Day followed day, and night followed night in a weary monotony that gradually dulled the edge of

Mark's anguish. He learned to walk carefully so that he would not be struck by the deadly rattlesnake. He learned a few words of Spanish, and used them often because each time he did the faces of Jaime and Rosa María became pleased and proud.

Gradually his skin grew darker, and strength returned to his wiry body. In the light of day, he found it possible to forget, though he still woke at night, sweating and sometimes screaming at the horror of his dreams. Whatever he did, Rosa María would come to him as to one of her own and hold him gently in her arms until he was comforted.

Again there was lively interest in his eyes as he walked across the land. He learned to identify the track of the desert's creatures and to watch for them in the smoldering vastness.

They crossed the border and entered Sonora and now their steps hurried a little when they traveled and their stops for much-needed rest became fewer and of shorter duration.

At last, at dawn of the fourteenth day, they came over a mountain ridge and looked down at the tiny town of San Pablo.

It nestled in a narrow canyon, and contained no more than thirty small adobe buildings surrounding a plaza or village square. At one side of the plaza stood the Mission, with twin bell towers on either side of a weathered wooden cross.

A narrow stream wound through the town and down the valley beyond, which was green with small patches of growing things and dotted with tiny adobe houses in which the farmers lived.

Jaime Ortega and Rosa María and their two new sons went down the road to the town. They were seen long before they arrived and their friends and neighbors came out into the road to congratulate them on their safe journey, and to welcome them and their sons home.

Mark and León stood aside, embarrassed and shy at the strangeness of it all. But Jaime Ortega put a browned hand on each of their shoulders. He translated for Mark the excited Spanish of the townspeople.

Followed by a troop of townspeople and barefooted, half-naked children, they went to their house, which was one of the larger ones in San Pablo. Here, Rosa María happily built a fire upon the cold hearth. The neighbors brought in food and Rosa María cooked it.

They were home at last.

Chapter 3

MARK ATKINS, terrified by violence, was soon to learn that even San Pablo was not immune to it. Mistakenly, he thought he was safe from the Apaches and a repetition of their brand of terror.

He was wrong. Apaches were, it seemed, a condition of living in this remote place, just as were drought and flood, heat and cold. Each year in early fall they came swarming down out of the barren desert to raid and pillage, to plunder and kill.

As a direct result there were, in this village of a hundred and fifty-seven, only fifteen adult males, all the others having been killed over the years by raiding Apaches.

For the most part, the people of San Pablo accepted it philosophically. It was unchangeable, like the weather. When the Apaches came, they fought. Other times they lived, and worked, and gave birth and died.

The months of summer passed slowly and pleasantly. Mark and León went out into the surrounding hills by day and gathered wood or berries. Sometimes Mark went to the Mission and learned Spanish from the padre, who had long since approved Jaime Ortega's adoption of him. Because he wished to, he accepted and used the name Marcos Ortega, and he grew like a weed, his mind gradually finding peace.

But the time of raiding came, and a band of thirty Apaches swept along the valley one day, driving stolen horses and mules before them, killing all who resisted. When they had gone, seven of the people of San Pablo were dead. Four women and several children had been kidnapped.

The silver mine, back in the hills, where Jaime Ortega worked, was short three workers that could ill be spared. Two days later, the owner of the mine, Rafael Hernandez, set out on horseback to protest the Apache scourge to the Sonora government.

Many times had Señor Hernandez protested, always in vain. This time he gathered, as he went, other mine owners along his route. Together they gave the government an ultimatum: provide protection against Apaches or the mines will close.

As a result of their ultimatum, a practice begun many years before was renewed. The Sonora government offered a bounty for Apache scalps: a male scalp was worth a hundred pesos, a female scalp or a female prisoner brought seventy-five, and that of a child, or the child itself, was priced at fifty pesos.

A year passed. And for the first time in Jaime Ortega's memory, September passed with no Apache raids. Roaming the hills north of San Pablo were a score of gringos that worked the mountains of northern Sonora hunting Apaches in the way that other men will hunt for game.

Three of them came, one night when Mark was fourteen, into the streets of San Pablo. They came to Jaime Ortega's house, since it was one of the largest, to ask for food and lodging.

The big one, smelling of sage and grease and the smoke of campfires, spoke for them, doffing his hat gallantly to Rosa María and grinning raffishly at the two boys gawking behind her. "I'm Abe Healy, señora. This here's Greco Corbin, an' the redhead's Sam Smead. We been huntin' 'Paches back in the mountains an' we've run out of grub. We'd take it kindly if you'd feed us an' put us up for the night. In the mornin' we'll buy grub at the store."

Rosa María did not understand them, but when Mark translated for her she agreed graciously, and let them into the house. Jaime Ortega got up and came forward, bowing and smiling with native courtesy.

Healy kept glancing at Mark curiously. At last Jaime said proudly, "This is Marcos, señor. We found him two years ago when we traveled to Los Santos to get León, who is the son of my dead sister. Marcos's mother and father were killed by Apaches in a stage-coach raid. We have raised him, with León, as our own son."

Rosa María turned from the hearth, her face pink at her own temerity and said in Spanish with shy pride, "Both Marcos and León are good sons to us, señores. Never have I wanted for firewood since the day they came. They are like our own."

Jaime translated smilingly, and Mark flushed with pride.

Covertly he studied the three men because they were the first of his own race he had seen since coming to San Pablo.

Healy was a powerfully built tall man in his early twenties. His face and eyes were bold, and he wore a clipped beard. His skin, nearly as dark as Jaime Ortega's from exposure to the Sonora sun, was beginning to show fine lines around the eyes. He had a rough, natural charm that completely captivated Rosa María.

But Mark caught Jaime watching the three with some puzzlement in his eyes, and trepidation. After that, he studied them more carefully himself.

For a while, he saw nothing but Healy's charm, his rough good humor, his friendly ways. But before the evening was done, he had seen what Jaime Ortega had seen. Healy's eyes were hard as pieces of polished agate, in spite of the lines of humor that showed whenever he smiled or laughed.

Greco Corbin was shorter than Healy, but he was built like a bull. His face was swarthy and covered with a short stubble of blue-black whiskers. His eyes were green, as pitiless as those of a hunting cat.

The third, Sam Smead, was a slight and scrawny man, the oldest of the three. His face and neck were deeply seamed, and in each of the seams was an accumulation of dirt and campfire soot. Whenever he swallowed, his protruding Adam's apple bobbed noticeably.

All three were roughly dressed and carried a smell of wildness about them compounded of sage and smoke and dust and sweat. And they had another thing in common—each wore a cartridge-studded leather belt around his waist, and sagging from this belt, a holstered, deadly Colt's revolver.

Supper was a noisy, hilarious business, and when it was over the three Americanos, and Jaime, and Mark and León, went out to stable the visitors' horses.

Jaime seemed unnaturally quiet, and this puzzled Mark. He stood back in the soft, warm shadows and watched as the gringos threw off their saddles and unpacked their pack animals.

A strange smell seemed to pervade the air, one that

was neither horse smell nor that of the three bounty hunters, yet one that made Mark's neck prickle and stirred vague uneasiness in him.

Healy and his two companions laughed and joked incessantly. Greco Corbin took a brown bottle from his saddlebags and passed it around. Jaime Ortega tipped it politely when it was offered him and afterward choked and coughed as though he would never stop.

When the horses were stabled, the three returned to the gallery.

They finished their bottle and lighted the *cigarros* which Jaime gave them. They grew more talkative and more noisy. Healy got a second bottle from his saddlebags and they quickly finished that.

By their talk, Mark gathered that they were through hunting for a time and were heading south to collect their bounties. Jaime inquired courteously if they had been successful and Healy threw back his head and shouted with laughter. "Show him, Greco!" he bellowed.

Jaime protested, his face turning pale. But Healy would not be stopped. He went with Greco to the stable and when they returned, each carried a canvas sack. They dumped the sacks triumphantly onto the hard-packed gallery floor.

At once the smell that had so puzzled Mark returned, stronger than ever now. Again he felt the crawling sensation on the back of his neck. An unexplainable feeling of horror came over him. His body began to tremble. He closed his eyes, and seemed to hear the shrill cries of attacking Apaches. He breathed, and again he smelled blood and death, mingled this time with the smell of the Apaches themselves.

Healy shouted proudly, "Here's some 'Pache sons of bitches that won't be raidin' your town no more, Ortega!"

Jaime's breath drew in audibly. In the darkness he crossed himself before he asked almost breathlessly, "How many, señores?"

"Thirty-seven, by God, countin' the squaws an' kids."

"You have the scalps of children there?" Horror was in Jaime Ortega's voice.

Healy peered at him angrily in the semi-darkness. "Why not? Hell, they kill your kids, don't they?"

Jaime shook his head. "Not often. Sometimes they steal them, but seldom do they kill them."

Mark stared at Healy's face. He thought he would remember its evil ugliness forever. With an almost inaudible cry, he turned and ran into the darkness.

He did not stop until he was high on the hillside. Then he sat down, trembling and exhausted. He stared down at the dim lights of the town below, trying to still the confusion in him.

He hated Apaches. Why, then, should he hate men who hunted and killed Apaches? Because they killed Apache children? Or because they killed for a bounty, the way men hunt wolves and other predators?

He didn't know. He heard sounds below him and tensed, but it was only León, panting heavily as he climbed toward him.

León carried blankets and food. Jaime had sent him and had told him it would be all right if the boys spent the night on the hillside.

León sat down beside him and gave him some tortillas he had brought along, but Mark could not eat.

León asked puzzledly, "Why did you run away, Marcos?"

Mark shook his head and didn't answer.

"Was it the scalps, Marcos? They did have a strong, strange smell, did they not?"

Mark's stomach churned, remembering that smell. He said, "It was not only the scalps."

"Was it the Americanos then? Why, Marcos? They are your own people, your own kind."

Mark said violently, "Not my kind, León!"

"Do you not wish to be like them? Ah, to wear a belt studded with cartridges and one of the revolving pistols! To ride a fine horse. That would be a thing, Marcos!"

Mark said bitterly, "And kill Apache children for money?"

"One would not have to kill children."

Mark laid down and pulled a blanket over his head. He muttered, "I do not wish to talk about it."

León settled down near him, wrapped in another blanket, and promptly went to sleep.

Mark did not sleep for a long time. He did not

understand himself. If one hated Apaches, as Mark surely did, he should rejoice when they were killed.

He remembered the way Jaime Ortega had looked when the Americanos dumped out their sacks of scalps. Jaime hated the Apaches too, surely. Yet Jaime's feelings at seeing the scalps had been much the same as Mark's own feelings.

But he wearied of confusion after a time and closed his eyes. Eventually he went to sleep.

In the morning, when he awoke, the Americanos had gone.

Chapter 4

SOUTH into the region of Sonora rode the trio of Americans. It had been a good year, and Abe Healy was pleased. He carried thirty-seven Apache scalps in the two canvas sacks. He had counted them up, putting them into separate piles for male scalps, female scalps and children's scalps. He figured they'd bring 2,400 pesos. Added to the 1,900 the group had already collected, that came to 4,300 pesos. As the leader, Healy got half. The remainder was to be split between Greco Corbin and Sam Smead.

It hadn't been easy, even though Healy had never attacked a party of more than half a dozen Apaches. Most of the scalps had been obtained in raids on small villages while the braves were gone. But a few had been taken the hard way, in combat with the braves themselves.

Three days south of San Pablo, they came to Hermosillo, the capital of Sonora, and rode through its narrow, twisting streets until they came to the building which housed the government. Here they dismounted and tied their horses. The three marched in and dumped out their sacks of grisly trophies on the paved floor of the anteroom.

Captain Ramón Vigil wrinkled his nose with distaste, staring first at the bits of hide and hair on the floor, then at the three dirty, unshaven men before him.

Healy wiped his hands on the legs of his pants and said, "I make it twenty-four hundred pesos, Captain. Pay up."

The captain shook his head. "The regulation has been changed, señores, I am sorry to say. The bounties have been lowered. Fifty pesos for male scalps, thirty-seven and a half for female and twenty-five for those of children. You have twelve hundred pesos coming."

He called an assistant and directed him to pay the money.

Healy and his two companions argued long and bitterly. Their eyes turned ugly and their faces flushed, but the captain was adamant, finally saying disgustedly, "Take your money and go, señores. I will take no more abuse from you. Continue, and I will imprison you. The Apache raids have almost stopped. The bounties were set too high. The government cannot afford to continue paying such high bounties."

Healy snatched the heavy sack of silver from the captain's desk. He looked the captain straight in the eye and snarled, "You'll be sorry for this, you renegin' son of a bitch! Your whole damn Mex government is goin' to be sorry!"

The captain flushed, not understanding the English words but understanding very well Healy's expression and manner. He raised his voice to call his guards, but Healy turned and stamped out, followed by his companions.

None of them took it well. Greco Corbin looked at Healy as though he were wondering if Healy had made some sort of deal previously with the captain. Healy snarled at him, "I know what you're thinkin', damn you. But don't ever say it."

Greco scowled and looked away. Sam Smead said, "Don't start fightin' amongst yourselves. Thing to do is think this out."

"Think it out!" snarled Healy. "What the hell's to think out? We been cheated an' that's all there is to it."

"Mebbe not," said Smead secretively. "Mebbe not. Let's get us a drink an' think on it."

They proceeded to the nearest cantina. Healy was in a brooding, sour mood that only grew worse with the liquor he drank. Corbin kept pace with him and with each drink, his obvious suspicion of Healy increased. Smead drank less than half the drinks the others did. His drinking seemed to improve his disposition. A smile lingered on his thin, pale lips and deepened the creases around his mouth.

Once Healy snapped irritably at him, "What the hell you grinnin' at?"

"An idea I got. Come on. Let's ride an' I'll tell you about it."

They rode out, heading north. Healy led, setting a fast pace, and occasionally looking behind as though expecting pursuit.

When they were safely away and into the mountains again, Healy pulled up and let the others come alongside. "Now, what's this idea you got?" He was obviously in a better humor now.

Smead said, "There's a way to make up what we got cheated out of today. A hell of a lot easier way than huntin' them damn wild Apaches."

Both Healy and Corbin waited expectantly. Corbin stared at Smead suspiciously, Healy doubtfully.

Smead grinned as though enjoying their suspense. After a few moments, he said, "A dark-haired scalp is a dark-haired scalp, ain't it? How's that damn captain goin' to know what kind of critter it comes off of?"

Healy's eyes brightened. "You mean go after friendly Injuns?"

Smead shrugged expressively. "That ain't exactly what I had in mind. I was thinkin' of Mexicans."

Healy whistled.

Smead said, "It'll be like shootin' fish in a barrel. We can take fifty or a hundred scalps out of a single town. We make us a big haul an' take 'em south fast before the news reaches the capital. We collect our bounty an' get the hell out."

Corbin began to chuckle. Healy's broad face split into a wide grin. "What the hell are we waitin' for? Let's get started."

Smead shook his head. "Not so fast. There's soldiers in this part of the country, an' news travels fast. Thing to do is to go north somewhere, 'way back in the mountains. Pick a small village that's off the beaten track."

Healy thought about that for a moment. "Like San Pablo."

"Yeah. Like San Pablo."

Healy automatically took out his knife and began to whet it on a small stone. He put it away, then fished in his saddlebags and took out a bottle. He passed it to Smead and Smead took a long drink.

They continued to ride and to pass the bottle back and forth. If there had been any doubts or stirrings of conscience in Abe Healy, the liquor stilled them. Hell, a smart man didn't let himself be cheated.

He began to laugh uproariously. "Only one thing wrong with this," he choked.

"What's that?" asked Corbin, grinning.

"We ain't goin' to be able to see that captain's face when he finds out he's been had."

The day passed, and by nightfall they were nearly thirty miles north. They stopped in a small village and bought several more bottles and then went on to camp beyond the town.

Healy kept drinking steadily. There seemed to be a

compulsion in him to drink tonight. Long after the others were sleeping, he still sat and stared into the fire. Occasionally he took a long drink from the bottle.

He thought of Captain Vigil and the reduced bounty. He thought of the risks they had taken in obtaining the Apache scalps. By God, it would be different this time. This time there'd be no risk.

Eventually, he drank himself into unconsciousness, and awoke in the morning with a foul-tasting mouth and a splitting headache.

He took a long drink immediately upon getting up, and it eased the headache and quieted his nerves. He spiked his coffee heavily, and ate but little with it.

Corbin and Smead were in high spirits, but Healy's mood got only worse as the day progressed. His drinking continued, and they rode out of their way in late afternoon to replenish their liquor supply.

Healy kept himself in a kind of alcoholic daze all that evening, growing more broody and more morose with each passing moment. In common with many other Americans who lived on the frontier, Healy did not consider Indians human at all. They were wild animals that preyed alike on whites and other, more peaceful Indians. They were game to be hunted and killed. Therefore, killing them had not bothered his conscience at all.

But this was different, and he drank to forget the difference. When his mind dredged up mental images of Jaime Ortega, his wife Rosa María and the two young boys, he shuddered and forced his thoughts into other channels.

But in spite of his drinking, in spite of his efforts not to think of what they were going to do, tension increased in him as they approached San Pablo. Smead and Corbin began to watch him suspiciously and with distrust. Once Corbin said disgustedly, "What the hell's eatin' you, Abe? Lay off that damn liquor. We'll be in San Pablo tonight and we don't want to get there stinkin' drunk or it'll be our own scalps that get took instead of a bunch of Mexican scalps."

Healy snarled at him, "Mind your own goddam business, you son of a bitch! Don't talk to me like that!"

Corbin remained silent after that, but his eyes were virulent. Smead looked at Healy appraisingly, and with a small smile on his thin lips. It was as though Smead looked into his thoughts, and Healy hated him for it.

He made up his mind he wouldn't touch any more liquor. He needed his wits about him when they reached San Pablo.

He rode for almost an hour without reaching into his saddlebags. His head began to ache terribly. His hands began to shake. Nerves in his body jumped erratically. His muscles twitched.

He dropped behind, and when he was out of sight of the others, withdrew the bottle from the saddlebags and took a long drink. Afterward, he spurred and caught up.

Slowly the sun dropped behind the mountains in the west. Dusk came down upon the land, and they topped the last rise and looked down into San Pablo.

Smead and Corbin dismounted. Both watched Healy as he slid heavily from his saddle.

He forced a certain clarity to his mind. He said harshly, "We'll wait here until most of the lights are out. Then we'll head on in. Use your knives as much as possible. We don't want to make any more noise than we have to or we'll have the whole town down around our ears. Don't shoot unless you have to to save your lives."

Smead drawled, "We goin' to separate?"

Healy shook his head. "Too dangerous. We'll stick together and work one house at a time."

They sprawled on the ground to wait. Smead closed his eyes and went to sleep. Healy looked at him, hating such nerves of iron. He studied Corbin and thought he detected a certain nervousness in the man.

For a few moments he considered talking to Corbin about calling the whole thing off—it was too dangerous. When the news of what they'd done got out every Mexican in Sonora would be hunting them. Troops from the capital would be riding on every road, in every canyon.

Then he discarded the idea. Both Corbin and Smead had been watching him strangely, as though they doubted his nerve.

He got up and took the bottle out of his saddlebags,

holding it so that Corbin couldn't see. He walked behind a cedar and took a long, slow drink.

Then he sat down in the darkness to wait.

On the night that Healy and his two companions arrived at the edge of San Pablo, Mark and León were far back in the hills more than five miles away. They had received permission from Jaime in the afternoon to take the burro and some food and blankets and camp out for the night. In the morning, they were going to gather piñon nuts along their route back to San Pablo, and load the burro with dry wood.

It was not the first time they had camped out, so Mark found it hard to understand the vague feeling of uneasiness that troubled him. He knew there was little chance that Apaches were in the country. Jaime would not have allowed them to go if he had thought there was any danger.

They built a small fire and, when it had died down, warmed beef tacos over the coals. They ate ravenously, but Mark's eyes constantly roamed the shadows beyond the fire.

León noticed and asked, "What is the matter, Marcos? Why do you watch the shadows?"

Mark grinned, and shrugged. "I was playing a game."

León brightened. "Let us be scalp hunters—" He stopped abruptly and said, "I am sorry, Marcos. I forgot that they upset you."

"They don't upset me. All right, let's be scalp

hunters." He frowned thoughtfully, quieting his uneasy nerves by force of will. "We are camped a mile from an Apache village. Tomorrow at dawn we will attack it and take many scalps. But we must watch carefully tonight or their scouts may find us."

León began to kick dirt on the fire. Mark was glad when its light died out. Now, at least, León would be unable to see his face, unable to see his uneasiness.

He followed Leon's words with half his mind, and played out his part of the make-believe halfheartedly.

He puzzled at the feelings that troubled him, and because he had no answers, his uneasiness increased.

León tired of the game and wrapped himself in his blankets. Soon he was sleeping peacefully. But Mark lay awake, listening to the night sounds. . . .

When dawn began to streak the sky, Mark got up immediately and built a fire. He warmed their breakfast over the coals and woke León. While León ate, he loaded the burro with their blankets and remaining food. Daylight hadn't dispelled his worry. The only thing that could do that, he knew now, was to get back to San Pablo.

It was almost midmorning when they topped the ridge behind the town and looked down into its streets. The town should have been quiet, with the men away working in the mine. Instead, the streets were filled with people, standing in small groups, talking.

A low, ominous murmur arose through the clear air,

a sound neither León nor Mark had ever heard before. It increased Mark's uneasiness, and made a sudden chill run down his spine. Something had happened; something terrible had happened.

León said in a small, tight voice, "What is it, Marcos? What is happening?"

Mark shrugged. He felt older and bigger than León. He said hoarsely and impatiently, "We will not know until we go find out."

León began to run down the slope. Mark followed, dragging the burro, and beset by a nameless fear.

The padre Father Vicente, standing at the door of the mission, was first to see them. He left the mission at once, crossed the stream and climbed quickly toward them. He intercepted them while they were still fifty yards from the bottom of the hill.

He stood squarely in their path, a tall, gaunt man with deep-set, patient eyes. There was sadness in his face. Suddenly Mark wanted to cry. He asked hesitantly, "What is it, Padre? Have Apaches . . ."

Father Vicente shook his head. Mark saw anger in the padre's eyes, and it puzzled him. He had never seen anger in the padre before. Father Vicente said, "Not Apaches, my sons. Not Apaches. But we have been attacked. God be praised that we discovered them when we did."

Mark tried to push past him, but the padre restrained him with firm hands. Mark looked up into his face, knowing surely now that something had happened either to Jaime Ortega or Rosa María. His lips formed the word, "Jaime?" questioningly, and Father Vicente nodded. Mark's voice came out shrilly, "Rosa María?"

"Yes, my sons. Both of them."

"Who did it?" Mark could feel tears close, behind his eyes like floodwater crowding against a dam. He swallowed and clenched his teeth and repeated, "Who did it?"

"Think not of who did it, my son. Pray instead for those who are dead."

Mark jerked away from the padre's gentle hands. His voice was high and childish, but it was cold as ice. "Who did it, Padre?"

Father Vicente looked at him long and with much sadness. At last he replied with a little shrug, "It was the three scalp hunters who visited San Pablo several nights ago. Come now, we will pray."

But Mark shook his head. "Why did they do it?"

A shudder shook the priest's gaunt frame. He looked at Mark closely for a moment. His voice was reluctant and very low. "For money, my son. For a bounty. They seem to have discovered that a scalp from one of our people cannot be told from the scalp of an Apache. May God have mercy on their souls!"

Mark's face went white with shock. León sat down and began to cry almost hysterically. Mark looked up at the padre. "Yes, Padre. God must have mercy on their souls. Because I never will."

Chapter 5

THERE was a change in Mark Atkins, a change the townspeople found it hard to understand.

He was told how the scalpers came in the night, how they entered three houses and killed their occupants before they encountered resistance. In the fourth house, a man named Felipe Rodriguez shot at them with an old musket, wounding one in the arm.

Immediately they all shot back, killing Rodriguez with their first volley of shots, killing his wife immediately afterward.

But the shots aroused the town and, fearing it was an Apache attack, the townspeople came running into the streets, carrying the first weapons they could lay their hands on.

The scalpers fled, demoralized by the unexpected resistance. They escaped, heading north for the border, but not before they had been recognized.

Mark heard the story, his face white and without expression. His eyes shed not a single tear, even as he stood at the graveside later and listened to the padre pray over Jaime and Rosa María.

The townspeople, and especially the padre, watched him with bewildered compassion. They knew the story of the death of his parents. They knew how fond he had been of both Jaime and Rosa María. Why, then, did he not grieve? Why did he not cry?

León was adopted by a cousin of Jaime's. But Mark

refused to live with them, or indeed with anyone. So Father Vicente kept him at the Mission, trying always to reach his withdrawn mind, always failing.

A week passed. And at last, one night, León heard a soft call from outside his window, and, going to see who it was, found Mark with a bundle slung over his back.

Mark whispered expressionlessly, "I have come to say good-by."

León began to tremble in his thin cotton nightshirt. "Where are you going?"

"After the murderers of Jaime and Rosa María."

Excitement was strong in Leon's voice. "What will you do when you find them?"

"Kill them."

León scoffed, "You are only a boy, no bigger than I."

"But I will grow. I am taking Jaime's burro. Tell the padre I have taken him. Someday I will send you the money to pay for him."

León said grandly, "He is yours."

Mark came close to the window. He reached out and squeezed León's arm. "Good-by, León." His voice trembled slightly.

"Good-by, Marcos."

Mark turned and disappeared into the darkness. He found the placid old burro tied to a tree where he had left him. He mounted and beat a tattoo with his heels against the burro's sides. The animal turned his head to look at Mark reproachfully, then walked through the sleeping town and out onto the road leading north.

Mark could feel Jaime Ortega's old muzzle-loader beneath his knee. But the gun could not dispel the coldness that lay like a ball of ice in the pit of his stomach. Nor could it dispel the fear that came to him at each small noise beside the road.

He rode steadily until daylight, and then stopped to water the burro at a narrow stream. He drank a little himself and ate a tortilla from his meager hoard. Then, reassured by the light of day, by the sun climbing into the sky, he lay down in the shade and closed his eyes.

He knew he was being foolish and reckless. He knew the chances were poor that he'd ever reach civilization. He would try to take the route Jaime had taken two years before, and he would try to find the waterholes at which Jaime had filled his canteens, but he could not be sure he would. Nor could he be sure he would not be caught and killed by Apaches.

Fear worse than any he had ever known suddenly knotted his stomach. It made his hands tremble and made his mouth dry as cotton.

He could go back now; it was not too late. But how could he face León and admit he had lacked the courage to back up his boast?

He got up angrily. Though traveling on the road was easier, he deliberately left it now, aware that there might be pursuit, and rode in the timber, guiding himself by the sun by day, by the stars when night came down.

Exhausted by the trip, he began to doubt his own capabilities. Jaime had taken two weeks to journey from the place at which he had found Mark, to San Pablo. It must be a distance of nearly a hundred and fifty miles.

But he could not go back. He would not go back. Better to die of thirst in the desert, trying, than to go back and live with the knowledge that he had failed Jaime and Rosa María. He was fourteen. It was time to stop being a boy and begin to be a man. . . .

Night followed night and day followed day in a seemingly endless procession. Mark's small store of food ran out, but he managed to stun a rabbit with a rock. He killed it and skinned it, and broiled it over a fire. He ate one hind quarter and put the rest away, though the hunger in him was overpowering enough to have devoured it all and still wanted for more.

Hunger was a thing that lived with him constantly now, until he lost sight of the reason for his journey and thought only of food. But he went on doggedly.

He came to the edge of the mountains on the fifth day and dropped down onto the desert, where traveling was faster and less tiring. But he stayed close to the range of mountains on his left, knowing that only in the mountains would he find water. He learned to watch their barren faces, learned to know where the water would most likely be. He watched the ground for the tracks of game, and sometimes followed their trails to tiny seeps of water high in some rocky gulch.

Now, he slept longer and oftener, and traveled less. The weakness in him grew. He spent the entire eighth day hunting for something he could kill and eat. He found nothing.

Despair invaded his thoughts. Even the burro grew weak and ceased to graze.

On the twelfth day, the burro laid down at sunrise and did not get up again. When Mark went to him in the afternoon, dully and without interest, the burro was dead.

Mark slumped beside him and wept with despair. He was beaten—finished. He would never reach civilization. He would die here in the desert, alone.

But out of despair came a revelation that would have been impossible without it. The burro was not only transportation, not only a loved and pampered friend—the burro was food. He was meat that could now, in desperation, be eaten even though the eating would make Mark feel like a cannibal.

Conquering his revulsion, he skinned out one of the burro's hind legs. He could not cut loose the bone, so he cut chunks of meat from the leg and laid them carefully on a rock. Then, risking Apaches, he built a big fire.

All night, he broiled chunks of meat on sticks over the fire, knowing that if he did not they would be rotten before he could consume them. Afterward he laid them back on the flat rock to cool.

He ate voraciously and, near dawn, slept soundly and peacefully for the first time. Fortunately, there were no Indians close enough to see the fire or to smell its smoke.

Next day, carrying all the meat he could, Mark continued his journey afoot.

The strength the meat had given him evaporated during the long hours of walking, the unaccustomed expenditure of strength. Too late, he knew that he had made a mistake, perhaps a fatal one. He should have stayed in San Pablo until he was older, until he could travel north with others that were coming this way.

Yet now he could not go back. He was closer to his destination than he was to San Pablo.

Time ceased to have meaning for Mark. He lost count of the days. He lived in a blazing hell of heat and thirst and numb desperation.

What kept him going, he could not have said. Perhaps it was nothing more than the age-old instinct of self-preservation. Perhaps it was more. Perhaps vengeance had become more important to him than life itself.

Eighteen days after leaving San Pablo, Mark stumbled upon a stage road and collapsed beside it. There, the crew of an eastbound stage found him at dawn.

Ross McKinley was a big, hairy man in his early forties. He hauled in instinctively on the lines when he saw the ragged form beside the road, then let them out immediately to slap the backs of the teams. He turned to the guard and shouted over the noise of the coach, "Whaddaya make of it? 'Pache trick?"

The guard's eyes roamed the terrain nervously. He shifted his shotgun warily and shrugged.

"Wantta risk a stop?"

Again the guard shrugged. He yelled, "You're the boss. But there could be fifty 'Paches out there."

The coach drew closer to the still form beside the road. McKinley thought he saw the figure stir.

Suddenly he hauled back angrily on the lines. He yelled, "Jump down and sling him inside. I think he's still alive. Gimme that damned shotgun. I'll cover you."

The coach rattled to a stop. The guard jumped down. McKinley's eyes roved the land nervously.

The guard called up, "He's alive! Hell, Ross, it's a kid. A white kid!"

"Get 'im inside an' take care of 'im. An' let's get the hell out of here."

The guard lifted Mark, astonished at his light weight. He laid him inside the coach and climbed in with him. The coach started up and rumbled east along the dusty road.

There was only one passenger this trip, a tired-looking woman. Her husband had been killed by Apaches and she was returning to her relatives in the East.

She took over at once, and the guard called out for the driver to stop again so that he could get back up on the box.

Mark was left alone in the coach with the woman, who dampened a cloth with water and began to sponge his face with it. After a time he opened his eyes and she lifted his head and poured a little water into his mouth.

He revived rapidly after that. She gave him a stale meat sandwich and he ate it ravenously.

"What's your name, youngster?" she asked when he had finished.

"Marcos, uh, Mark Atkins."

"What you doin' way out here?"

He eyed her suspiciously and did not answer. She shrugged wearily. "Suit yourself. It's no skin off my nose."

The coach rumbled on interminably and the heat of day increased. The woman lapsed into silence.

After a time Mark slept again, and when he woke they were pulling into a stage depot for a change of horses.

He remembered the place vaguely as the one at which the coach containing him and his parents had stopped before the attack two years before.

It was really a small settlement. There was a long, adobe building that housed the stage station and the agent's quarters. There was a large corral behind this building containing about two dozen horses. Outside the corral was a stack of hay, and through a corner of the corral wound a narrow, shallow stream. Beside it stood a single, monstrous cottonwood.

Across the road from the stage station was another adobe building. It housed a trading post and saloon in the front part. Two wings made a U of the building, each containing several tiny rooms which opened upon a courtyard behind the main part of the building.

In addition to these two large buildings, there were five or six adobe houses scattered haphazardly along the course of the stream.

The coach drew up and Ross McKinley helped the woman down and then peered in at Mark, "Feelin' better, ain't you?"

Mark nodded.

"Got any folks?"

Mark shook his head.

"What you gonna do?"

Mark hadn't thought about that. His mouth pinched together and at last he said defiantly, "I can get me a job, can't I?"

McKinley looked at him appraisingly. "You're some puny, you are." His eyes were not unkind.

Mark said, "I'm stronger than I look." His gray eyes met those of the driver steadily.

McKinley studied him a moment more, and then grinned. "I reckon you are at that. Come on. I got an idea I can fix you up."

Mark climbed down from the coach. McKinley strode off across the road toward the trading post, and Mark followed. There were several saddle horses racked before the place. Apparently this was a haven for all kinds of travelers.

Mark began to hope feverishly that he could somehow stay on here. It was the kind of place at which many travelers would stop, teamsters, cowhands, soldiers, perhaps even scalpers. Sooner or later Healy and his companions might come through here. And even if they didn't, sooner or later someone would come who knew them and knew where they were.

McKinley stopped just outside the door. He looked down at Mark. "Dawson, the man that runs this place, had an old Mex handyman that died about a week ago. I reckon maybe he'll let you take his place if you ain't afraid to empty spittoons an' fetch firewood an' carry out slopjars. They'll be other things to do too, like sweepin' an' carryin' water an' such. Wantta try it?"

Mark nodded. McKinley said, "You'll get your grub an' a place to sleep. Dawson's tighter than a vir . . . Well, he's tight, that's all."

He went in and Mark followed.

Mark had grown several inches taller in the two years he'd spent in San Pablo, but he hadn't filled out much. He was still thin and stringy.

His face had grown more angular, had lost its childish roundness. His cheekbones were high above his hollow cheeks. His eyes were gray and steady, his mouth firm and his lips compressed.

Dawson was a short, fat man in a dirty leather apron. He stood behind the bar, bearded and formidable, but he grinned widely when he saw McKinley, and poured the driver a drink without being asked. "Who's your friend, Ross?" His voice was a harsh rumble.

"Kid I picked up on the desert. Says he's got no folks. Says he wants a job. I figured maybe he could take Juan's place."

Dawson studied Mark critically. "Looks puny."

Mark flushed, but his eyes didn't waver from Dawson's. Dawson's expression altered subtly. He said, "What *you* got to say, boy?"

Mark said, "I'll earn my keep."

The corners of Dawson's mouth twitched, but he didn't smile. He gestured toward the rear of the building. "Rooms back there are all empty. Clean 'em up."

Mark hesitated, his eyes blank. Dawson came from behind the bar and got him a broom. Mark went out into the courtyard and entered the first of the tiny rooms.

He was ravenously hungry, and thirsty too. He was near exhaustion from his ordeal on the desert. But he conquered his weakness and worked all through the long afternoon. He swept. He emptied slopjars. He filled ollas with water from the well. It was dark when he had finished.

Dawson came out with a lamp and went from room to room, inspecting like a cavalry officer. When he had finished, he looked at Mark with approval. "You got you a job, boy. Now come on in and eat. After that, you sleep."

Mark followed him inside and sat down to eat. Dawson brought him the food and sat down opposite to watch him eat.

Dawson's eyes were curious and speculating, but he asked no questions, and Mark was grateful. He intended to tell no one why he was here, why he had been alone on the desert or where he had come from. Grown people were funny; you could never tell what they were going to do. Usually they figured a way to force you into the very thing you didn't want to do. If Mark let his mouth run off, first thing you knew he'd be headed east with someone or other that had promised to give him a home.

Mark ate sparingly, remembering the way his stomach had of rebelling when overloaded after a long spell without food. Finished, he followed Dawson into the courtyard. Dawson gave him the room closest to the saloon, where he'd be handy to his work.

When he left, Mark laid down fully dressed upon the bed and did not wake until Dawson pounded on the door at dawn.

The days and months passed in monotonous succession. Men came off the desert and paused briefly at Dawson's before going on. Mark scrutinized them all with impassive eyes and an expressionless face. Sometimes he questioned them as to whether they knew the scalpers, but always his questions drew negative answers.

Hard work and plenty of food did wonders for him. He grew taller and his body filled out with strong, wiry muscles. His skin grew dark from the desert sun. Fuzz began to grow on his jaws and chin.

Dawson tried many times to draw him out as to why he sought Healy and Corbin and Smead, but Mark refused to talk about it. He did his work and was cheerful. But whenever the conversation drifted around to himself and his past, he withdrew from it.

When he was fifteen, Dawson gave him an old Navy Colt's that he'd taken from a drifter for a night's drinking spree. And thereafter, when his work was done, Mark could be found either in his room, practicing drawing and snapping the empty gun, or out on the desert half a mile behind the saloon, firing it at tin cans set upon the rim of an arroyo.

Because he feared he would lose the boy, who was the best worker he'd ever had, Dawson began to pay him fifteen dollars a month, little dreaming that the money would be the means of his eventually losing the very thing he sought to keep. And Mark, with a wisdom beyond his years, saved it carefully against the time when he would leave, spending only enough of it for powder and ball to fire the Colt's revolver five times every day.

At eighteen, Mark was almost six feet tall, and weighed over a hundred and forty pounds.

His face was calm, and singularly without expression. But he had never forgotten. Each night he had been at Dawson's, except for the very first, he had taken a moment before going to sleep to visualize in his mind the faces of Healy and Corbin and Smead. Then he would remember those of Jaime Ortega and Rosa María.

Time dimmed the faces but did not eradicate the ritual. When Mark could no longer remember the faces of the scalpers, he repeated their names. He'd know them when he saw them, and that was enough.

Eventually, even the ritual of remembering ceased to have real meaning, but he clung to it with a tenaciousness approaching desperation. It was the purpose of his life, this vengeance. If he lost it, he'd be left with nothing.

His hand grew fast with the Navy Colt's, his eye more accurate. His body grew taller and stronger, and the little leather sack he kept in his bunk grew heavy with gold. He was almost ready to start his search in earnest. All he needed was something to set him on his way.

Chapter 6

ON ONE of those gray, misty days so seldom seen in the desert, Mark came into Dawson's from his stint of daily target practice. His thoughts were occupied, and he forgot, for once, to remove his gun and belt.

It was early afternoon. At the bar were five men, three of whom had been there all day. Two were strangers, having come in separately less than an hour before.

Mark picked up a broom and began to sweep. He glanced, from habit, at the men at the bar. One bore a slight resemblance to Sam Smead from behind, but where he turned, Mark realized at once that the resemblance was only superficial.

Mark wore thin cotton trousers, frayed at the bottom, and a thin cotton shirt. He wore straw sandals and a straw sombrero. The cartridge belt and holstered gun around his middle looked a bit ridiculous.

The red-haired man, the one Mark had thought resembled Smead, did not immediately turn back to the bar. Instead he kept watching Mark. A small, odd smile twisted his thin lips.

Mark ignored him after that first brief glance. He continued to sweep.

Talk ran along the bar, idle talk from idle men. The red-haired man did not join in it. He downed several more drinks quickly, then swung again, leaning against the bar with both his elbows resting on its top.

Mark finished sweeping and brushed the dirt out the front door. Then he returned, heading around the bar to replace the broom.

Deliberately, grinning cruelly, the red-haired man stuck out a spurred and booted foot.

Mark sprawled to the floor. He got up and dusted himself off automatically. He put his level gray eyes on the red-haired man, and knew at once that it had been no accident. Anger stirred in him.

The grinning stranger swung his head to look at Dawson. "What's this, Dawson? A gunslinger down on his luck? Or a swamper fixin' to be a gunslinger?"

Dawson said flatly, "Neither. Just a kid that does his work and minds his own business. Let 'im alone."

"You mean he's dangerous? He don't look dangerous—just scared. A kid like him oughtn't to have a gun. He might hurt himself. Somebody ought to take it away from him."

Dawson said, "Don't try it. Just let 'im alone."

Mark felt a curious quickening of his blood, a light sensation in his head. He stood his ground, neither truculent nor frightened. Again he was struck by the resemblance between this man and Sam Smead.

His belly was jumping, but his hands were steady. The red-haired man studied him and chuckled contemptuously. "What kind of half-breed bastard is he anyhow? Half Mex and half Apache? Or half white and half Apache?"

Mark could feel his face flushing. He glanced at Dawson, who said irritably, "God damn it, Red, let 'im alone!"

Mark's own voice sounded strange in his ears. "No. Let's hear what's on his mind."

Red laughed aloud. "He talks, by God. Where'd he learn his English, Dawson, in the crib where his mother worked?" There was a steadying wickedness in Red's face and no sign that he would stop. Boredom had brought this on. Now, innate meanness and the liquor he had consumed would keep it going.

Mark controlled his anger with difficulty. He had been around Dawson's nearly four years now, long enough to have seen Red's type many times before, long enough to understand that the choice was his. He could take Red's calculated insults and walk away, alive and unhurt. Or he could, today, stop being a boy and become a man.

For a year now he had been hesitating on the brink of leaving, restrained only by the memory of his nearly disastrous trip north from San Pablo, a thing undertaken hastily and without adequate preparation. Here, he realized, was his chance to discover how ready he now was.

He could feel his heart beating hard and fast against his chest. He could feel a pulse in every part of his body. The lightness in his head increased until he almost seemed to be floating.

The oddest impulse came over him—he wanted to laugh. Perhaps it was partly hysteria, but the laugh, coming from his lips, did not sound hysterical.

Red's face flushed darkly. He stepped quickly away from the bar, letting his arms drop to his sides. There would be more words exchanged, but they would be only formalities. The words would be said and the challenge laid down. The swift, fleeting moment of death would come, the instant when the guns came out and billowed their clouds of smoke—

Dawson said sharply, "Red! God damn it!"

Red didn't turn again and Dawson reached under the bar for his shotgun.

Red's arms tensed in the odd way a rattler's body tenses before it strikes. And Mark knew suddenly, too late, that a vast gulf lies between drawing and shooting at a target and drawing and shooting at a man.

Half seen from the corner of Mark's eye, Dawson's shotgun cleared the bar. But Dawson couldn't shoot. Mark stood squarely in the line of fire.

The man next to Red was not so hampered. He seized the whisky bottle in front of him and brought it around in a vicious swing. It smashed on Red's head, drenching him with its contents, showering him with broken glass.

He staggered, reaching belatedly now for his gun. The man who had struck him kicked his hand and the gun went spinning across the floor. Red dived for it, then stopped, on hands and knees. For Dawson had laid his shotgun on the bar, its muzzle pointing down at Red. His voice was cold with anger. "Get up and get out of here, you son of a bitch!"

Red glared up at him balefully. He switched his glance to the man who had broken the bottle over his head. An odd change came over him. The fight went out of his face, but the anger remained, glowing in the depths of his narrowed eyes.

He got up, saying sullenly, "How about my gun?"

"Pick it up and get out."

Red stopped and picked up his gun. Shoving it back into its holster, he walked unsteadily to the door and went out without looking back.

Dawson began to grumble sourly, "Quarrelsome bastard! I oughtta let 'im have both barrels!"

Mark looked at the man who had struck Red. Reaction was setting in and he could feel tremors in his arms and legs. He grinned. "Thanks."

The man studied Mark with a small, half-smile. "Maybe you didn't need no help. What's your name, kid?"

Mark picked up the broom at his feet. He said, "Mark Atkins."

The man stuck out his hand, his grin widening. "I'm Chester Ewing. You didn't look scared."

Mark returned his grin ruefully. "I was, though." He stood there for a moment, not wanting to leave but embarrassed because he could think of nothing to say. A current of liking flowed back and forth between them, a curious, magnetic thing that sometimes springs up between two men who are much alike.

Mark turned away at last and returned the broom to its niche behind the bar. But as he went on with his work, he studied Ewing covertly.

There was little physical resemblance between them. Chester Ewing was not so tall as Mark, but he was considerably thicker through the shoulders and chest. His hair, pale and fine as silk, had thinned over his forehead until his scalp showed plainly through. His eyes were blue and penetrating, and there was an odd mockery in them that was matched by a mocking twist to his mouth whenever he smiled.

Excitement began to rise in Mark as he played with an unexpected idea that had begun to grow in his mind. He finished his work quickly, then went to his room at the rear of the saloon. He got out his small, heavy sack of gold from inside the straw mattress and hefted it in his hand.

He couldn't stay here at Dawson's forever. And what better time to leave than now?

Leaving his room, he hurried across the courtyard and went out the back gate. He circled Dawson's and crossed the road to the stage station. Excitement that was almost fear kept rising in him, but his mind was made up now, and would not be changed.

Much of his time had been spent here at the stage station in the past several months, so it took him no more than a few minutes to buy a horse and saddle. The questions of the way-station keeper he brushed aside with a nervous smile.

He saddled his newly purchased horse and mounted. Crossing the road, his glance swung north. The whole world lay before him. It was an unnerving thought.

Chester Ewing was still at the bar, but he was eating now, finishing up. Mark hesitated at the door. He had intended to ask Ewing if he could ride with him. Now he realized it would be an imposition, and Ewing would probably refuse.

Ewing paid for his meal, got up and swung toward the door. Mark stood aside, silent. Ewing grinned. "Good luck, kid."

"Thanks." Mark watched him leave, then turned resolutely toward Dawson. "It's time I left, Mr. Dawson. Will you sell me some supplies?"

Dawson scowled. "I knew this was comin'. It had to come. But why today?"

Mark shrugged. "Why not?" He swallowed, and

forced out the words, "You been mighty good to me. I . . ."

"To hell with that. You've paid your way. Don't ever think you haven't."

Mark dragged out his bag of gold, which was lighter now. "I need supplies."

Dawson's voice was harsh. "Put that away." He came from behind the bar, wiping his hands ineffectually on the leather apron that was shiny with grease. "Come on. I'll fix you up an outfit."

He found a pair of boots and tossed them to Mark. Gray wool pants followed, then an old Army shirt. Lastly, he found a slicker and a weatherbeaten, sweat-stained Stetson. He growled apologetically, "I'd give you new stuff, but this is better. The country's full of bastards like that damned Red. A new outfit's just an invitation to them."

Mark shucked out of his lightweight clothes and put on the new ones. A strange feeling of unreality possessed him. He'd been here so long it was going to be like leaving home.

Dawson watched him, scowling fiercely. Then he whirled, and dug among the shelves behind the counter. He got a couple of blankets and spread them on the counter. He went behind the bar to the kitchen and came back with some food, a coffeepot, skillet and a bag of coffee. He laid them on the blankets and rolled them up. Lastly, he got out a scarred Henry rifle in a saddleboot, and an old pair of saddlebags into which he put a couple of boxes of rim-fire cartridges for the rifle.

He thrust the stuff at Mark, then stood shifting heavily on his big, booted feet. Abruptly he stuck out his powerful hand. "Luck, boy. I know you're goin' hunting. I know you're hunting men. Guess it's none of my business why. If it was, you'd of told me. Anyhow, I hope you find 'em. An' I hope when you do, you can handle 'em. You . . . uh . . ." He cleared his throat uncomfortably. "You need anythin', you just get word to me. Hear?"

Mark nodded, silently shifted the gear and stuck out his hand. Dawson nearly crushed it. Then Mark whirled, his eyes burning, and rushed out the door.

He tied on his gear with shaking hands. Then, with a last look at Dawson's, he mounted and rode out north.

He rode blindly for half a mile. Questing back and forth, he picked up the trail of a single horseman—Ewing probably. He swung into it and rode ahead. Hell, all the man could do was say no.

The trail angled west, and in late afternoon climbed off the desert into the low, cedar-covered mountains. Mark knew he was entering Apache country now. It was not far from here that his parents had been killed. He rode carefully, his eyes watchful and alert. It suddenly occurred to him that instead of following Ewing's trail, he might be following Red's. The thought made a chill run up his spine.

At dusk, Mark stopped where the trail crossed a stretch of rocky ground, trying to make it out. He dismounted and, bending close to the ground, went on slowly. He started, straightened, and shot a hand to his gun when a sharp voice called out, "Hold it, mister. Raise your hands and let's have a look at you."

Mark relaxed, but he raised his hands as he was told. The voice had been Ewing's. Holding a rifle at the ready, Ewing came out of the rocks and approached. At ten feet, he stopped and exclaimed, "Hell, it's the kid from Dawson's! What the devil are you trailin' me for?"

Mark swallowed. Suddenly it became hard for him to explain. Whatever bond he had felt existed between himself and Ewing back there at Dawson's was gone. He cleared his throat uneasily. "I've been wanting to ride north. I just thought maybe . . ."

"You thought you could ride with me? Is that it?"

Mark nodded.

Ewing was silent for a moment. Then he began to laugh. Mark could feel his face and neck flushing. Anger colored his voice. "What's so damn funny? To hell with you. I'll go on by myself."

Ewing continued to laugh, but sobered after a few moments. "Simmer down, kid. It's just struck me funny. That's what a man gets for . . ." He chuckled. "Never mind. Maybe it won't hurt nothin'. Come on. My camp's over here. You wouldn't last a day out here alone."

Mark followed, still angry and humiliated. He picketed his horse out after letting him drink rain water from the rock basin beside which Ewing had camped.

Ewing had no fire, and it was full dark now, but Mark could feel his presence. Ewing packed and lighted his pipe and smoked it, his back to a rock.

Silently Mark dug into his blankets in the darkness and got out some of the food Dawson had given him. He ate it, then drank from the rock basin. He asked, "How'd you find this?"

"Birds. This time of year a man can travel all the way through this country without goin' near a water hole. Pays, too, if he's a mind to keep his hair."

Ewing did not add to his statement, and though Mark would have liked to talk some more, he did not do so. After a while, Ewing rolled himself in his blankets. Mark followed suit. . . .

Ewing was up at dawn, and Mark awoke to the small sounds he made saddling his horse. He got up at once and saddled his own. Again they ate cold food, and afterward mounted and rode out, Ewing in the lead, Mark following.

Ewing seemed thoughtful, almost morose. But when the sun came up, he began to open up, occasionally pointing out something, a pillar of dust out on the desert, the track of an unshod Apache pony crossing their trail. The bond Mark had felt back in Dawson's returned.

Before he quite realized what he was doing, he was telling Ewing of the Apache raid on the stagecoach and the death of his parents. He told him of San Pablo, and of the three scalpers who had killed Jaime and Rosa María. He told him of riding the burro north four years ago and how close he had come to dying in the desert.

When he had finished, Ewing looked at him with new interest. "An' you been there at Dawson's all this time, just waitin' till you was old enough to take the trail?"

Mark nodded, somehow abashed.

All day they rode due north. Occasionally Mark would catch Ewing watching him strangely. When they camped for the night, Ewing nodded toward Mark's holstered gun. "You any good with that?"

Mark flushed. "I don't know. I've practiced . . ."

"Let's see how fast you can draw."

Mark drew the gun swiftly. Ewing nodded. "Not bad for a kid your age. But not near good enough. Healy's no kid. Neither are the two that was with him. What'd you do if you'd run into one of 'em tomorrow?"

Mark didn't answer. Ewing studied him carefully for a moment. "I thought so. You'd try, and you'd be dead."

Mark didn't know what to say. It was true—he wasn't ready, not at all.

Ewing saw his look. "Hell, don't get down in the mouth about it. You can learn. We'll get busy on it right after supper. A kid that's wanted somethin' as long as you have ought to have a crack at it, at least."

They ate, still without building a fire. Afterwards, as the first grays of dusk dropped over the land, Ewing showed him how to wear his belt and holster.

He pared it carefully with his knife until it left gun-grips and trigger guard exposed. He got a bar of strong laundry soap from his saddlebags and soaped the leather until the gun slipped easily in and out. After that, he rigged a leather tie-down around Mark's leg.

Mark was surprised at how much it helped. He practiced steadily until it was time to sleep, with Ewing coaching him.

Next morning, Ewing delayed their departure by an hour to instruct Mark. "Even when you're practicin' your draw, don't forget there's more to it than gettin' your gun out first. Every time you draw, pick yourself an imaginary target. It's like pointin' a finger, only you're goin' to be pointin' a gun. Get used to it. Take an hour every night to practice, because no matter how fast you get, there'll always be someone, some-where, that's faster. Remember that!"

For a week, Mark never fired his gun. Northward they traveled, camping cold, watchful and alert. Morning and night, Mark practiced, while Ewing looked on critically. Mark must have drawn and snapped his gun a thousand times. But he could sense the improvement in himself. He could sense the approval in Ewing's eyes.

Yet as he improved, a shadow of doubt appeared in Ewing's face. At last he spoke his doubt. "You're a natural, all right. You're faster than me right now. And it's a temptation, bein' fast. Man gets so he likes the feel of seein' men go down in front of him. He feels big—powerful. And pretty soon he's a killer. Don't be that, Mark."

Mark didn't quite know what to say. At last he said, "I just want them three. No one else."

Ewing smiled. "Good. Don't change that idea and you'll be all right."

They went on and at last, judging they were safely out of Apache country, Ewing called a halt on the bank of a wide, muddy stream. There was a grove of cottonwoods near their camp, and every day for a week he took Mark there and gave him intensive training in shooting accurately. At the end of the week, both Mark's and Ewing's powder supply was exhausted, but Mark could hit a six-inch bull's eye at fifty feet four times out of five. Breaking camp, Ewing said with a touch of envy, "You're better than I am and you've learned all you can from me. The rest of it is up to you." His eyes were friendly.

Mark had not realized, until now, how very close they had become. Traveling together, talking, living close, had strengthened the bond he had felt that first day in Dawson's. It almost seemed as though Ewing was his father, the relationship had become that close.

Ewing packed his pipe and lighted it thoughtfully. "Just one more thing. If you ever get in a gunfight, there ain't goin' to be no time for doubt. Your mind's got to be made up before you touch your gun. I reckon it's a kind of moral question a man's got to settle inside himself before he draws. You got to know that when you shoot you're goin' to kill. If it ain't settled beforehand, you're goin' to be hesitatin' a part of a second when you'd ought to be squeezin' off the trigger."

Mark said, "When I face one of those three there won't be no doubt."

Ewing nodded. "All right. Next problem. How you figure on findin' them?"

Mark didn't know. "Keep going until I do, I guess."

"It's a hell of a big country. You might never find 'em."

"I'll find them." There was certainty in Mark. No country was too big to keep them away from him.

"You know anything but swampin' in a saloon?"

Mark shook his head.

"Well, you can't do that. You're too good with your gun. Sooner or later someone like Red would start ridin' you, and you'd shoot it out and they'd see how fast you are. After that there'd be half a dozen reputation hunters after you." He shook his head. "Uh-uh. You got to know somethin' else that'll earn you a livin' whilst you look."

Mark stared at him curiously.

"Come on," Ewing said. "Let's get ridin'. There's a cattle outfit up in northern New Mexico that I used to work for. It's spring an' they'll be takin' on hands. What do you say to goin' up there an' signin' on? Work through the summer and you've got a trade—one you can work at wherever you are."

Mark nodded gratefully, and grinned. "Sounds good to me."

Mounting, the two set out across the empty miles.

They stopped at a town called Albuquerque, a day's ride from the ranch Ewing had mentioned, to replenish their supplies. Here, while Mark roamed the streets looking anxiously at every face, Ewing proceeded to get roaring drunk in a saloon.

When Mark went after him at dark, he was unconscious on the sawdust floor. Mark got him into a chair and then sat down to wait patiently until he came to.

At midnight, Ewing stirred and raised his head. He grinned foolishly at Mark and said apologetically, "Don't know why I do that. Sometimes . . ."

Mark said, "Forget it." He helped Ewing out of the saloon and back to the hotel, where he collapsed, clothes and all, onto the bed. Mark watched him for a long time, realizing that it made him feel good to be able to help Ewing, even in this small way. Then he went to bed himself.

In the morning, Mark and a red-eyed, rueful Chester Ewing, rode out north along the road to 2-Bar Ranch.

Chapter 7

RIDING in to 2-Bar Ranch. Mark was disappointed. He had expected a ranch headquarters in keeping with the tremendous size of the ranch.

Headquarters ranch house was a low, adobe building of but two small rooms, nestled in a grove of ancient cottonwoods. Behind it stood a bunkhouse, also of adobe, that was fifty feet long and about thirty feet wide. To one side of the bunkhouse was a cook-shack about half that size, and behind both buildings was an enormous series of pole corrals in the center of which a windmill whirled dizzily in a stiff spring wind.

There were forty or fifty head of horses in the corral, and a handful of cattle. Half a dozen men squatted in in the sun against the wall of the bunkhouse, smoking and talking idly.

A couple of them greeted Ches warmly, and he hunkered down with them, exchanging good-natured jibes and exaggerating the things that had happened to him during the winter in Arizona.

He introduced Mark, and they eyed him briefly and with impassiveness. After fifteen or twenty minutes of talk, Ches got up and sauntered over toward the ranch house, nodding to Mark to accompany him.

The ranch foreman sat in the front room of the ranch house, his booted feet on a spur-scarred desk. There was no other furniture but one old horsehair sofa. The rest of the room was littered with supplies, saddle and worn clothing.

Ches grinned at the foreman, a big, bluff, grizzled man with a ruddy, good-natured face and sharp, shrewd eyes. "Mark, this here's Cass Clark. Cass, Mark Atkins."

Clark eyed the gun at Mark's thigh, then lifted his glance to study Mark's face. He looked back at Ches. "Want jobs?"

Ches nodded.

"The kid a good hand?"

"He'll make one."

Clark nodded. "Thirty and beans. I'll give your kid a week. If he can't pull his weight by then, I'll put him to fixin' corral and buildin' fence."

Ches grinned. "He'll pull his weight."

Clark studied Ches. He said, "All right. There's a roundup crew workin' up north along Comanche Creek. Cut out three head of horses apiece and get goin'. You can make it by dark."

Ches nodded, turned and went out, and Mark followed him to the corral. Ches roped himself three horses and haltered them, tying the halter rope of one to the tail of the next, until he had them in a string.

Mark was awkwardly trying to rope his own, and not succeeding. Ches took the rope from him and showed him how. Then he waited patiently more than half an hour until Mark had roped his three. Trailing three horses apiece, they rode out north.

It was the beginning of a week of pure hell for Mark. He was thrown five times the next morning, and, bruised and skinned, rode twelve hours straight that day, exhausting all three horses in the process. That night, for the first time in months, he failed to practice with his gun.

The second day was even worse than the first, for his body was sore, and every movement hurt. But he stayed with it doggedly. Ches helped him all he could.

Two weeks of exhaustion followed, but at the end of that time, when Cass rode in, the roundup foreman nodded approval of Mark. "He's a good kid. Ain't afraid to work and he learns fast. Leave him alone, Cass."

Mark overheard, and walked away feeling fine. Afterward, he redoubled his efforts to make a good hand. Before another two weeks had passed, he was doing his work well: he could rope a calf almost as skillfully as Ches could; he could head a bunch-quitting steer in the high brush and thick cedars, and he showed a special knack for finding cows that had shaded up with their new calves in some brush-choked ravine.

He was well liked for his responsible attitude toward his work, though none of the regular 2-Bar hands ever got very close to him, or indeed even tried.

And now, every night, remembering the reason he was here and what would come when this was done, he slipped off by himself into some brush pocket or draw and practiced with his gun.

Spring roundup ended at last, and summer came. The cattle were moved to their summer range high in the mountains, and the hands dispersed. Mark and Chester Ewing were assigned to an isolated cow camp until beef roundup would begin in the fall.

Mark had filled out during the spring. Heavy work, long hours and plenty of food had built lean, hard muscles in his shoulders, chest and thighs.

After roundup, line-riding was like loafing. Each day Ches rode out east from the cow camp, and Mark rode west. They'd ride, and scan the hills, occasionally pushing a few strays south, sometimes doctoring a cow with hoof-rot, sometimes branding a slick-eared calf that had been dropped since roundup ended.

Now, Mark had a great deal of time for thinking, and for practicing with his gun. But as the weeks wore on, Ches began to grow moody, irritable and restless. His temper grew short, and at times he brooded on the stoop of the cabin far into the night.

Mark himself grew restless, as though in sympathy with Ches. So when Cass Clark came riding through with a couple of men one day in late July, Mark got him alone and said, "Cass, Ches is about to go crazy. How about a couple of nights in town?"

"For him or for both of you?"

Mark shrugged. "For both of us if you can spare us. For Ches if you can't. I can hold this down alone for two or three days until he gets back."

Cass grinned. "Go on, the both of you. I'll leave Slim and Willie here until you get back." He hesitated a moment. At last he said, "Ches is a heavy drinker. Look after him, kid."

Mark nodded. Grinning foolishly he walked over to the cabin and gave Ches the news. Ches let out a whoop, his face creasing into a wide smile for the first time in days. "Well, for God's sake, stir your stumps. Lordy! I can taste that whisky runnin' down my throat already!"

They saddled up quickly, picked up their pay from Clark, and rode out at a gallop, heading for town.

Town was Rio Blanco, a collection of mud and frame buildings that reminded Mark vaguely of San Pablo. For some reason, as they rode down the dusty road toward the sleepy town, he was beset by an odd mixture of excitement and dread.

He grinned wryly at himself, knowing he would feel this same mingled excitement and dread on the edge of a hundred towns before he finished his search. It was like the excitement a prospector knows at the beginning of each new quest, like that a man long away from civilization feels when he knows he will soon hold a woman in his arms.

Ches spurred his horse to a hard run at the edge of town and hauled up in a cloud of dust before the first saloon. He had his horse tied by the time Mark pulled up. The change in him was miraculous. Grinning up at Mark, he said, "Ahhhhh! Come on! Come on!"

Mark laughed. "You go ahead. I'm going to eat. Then I'm going to look around town. I'll see you later."

Ches sobered slightly. "Forget it for a day. Forget your damned hunt."

Mark shook his head, smiling. "I can't, Ches. I've got to look around this town."

Ches studied him for a moment, then turned and stamped into the saloon alone.

Mark turned and rode along the street until he reached a restaurant. Purposely he ordered beef tacos, and eating them was like going home, except that they were not as good as the ones Rosa María used to make. Sitting there, homesickness and loneliness washed over Mark, settling like lead in his chest.

He ate leisurely, and when he had finished, went out and stabled his horse. Afterward he loafed through the streets of the town. At sundown he turned his steps toward the saloon where Ches had gone.

While still a hundred yards away, he heard a shot, muffled, but plainly a shot. Briefly he stiffened. Then, in spite of himself, he was hurrying, almost running, toward the saloon. Through his mind ran Clark's words, "Ches is a heavy drinker. Look after him, kid."

In his heart, suddenly, was the same cold, nameless fear he had felt as he and León made their way down the slope toward San Pablo the morning of Jaime's and Rosa María's death. It was as though premonition had touched him, had told him Chester Ewing was somehow involved with the shot he'd heard.

Ches! Ches, who was like father, brother, teacher, all rolled into one. Mark's face twisted, as though at some physical pain. Then he burst through the saloon doors, almost tearing them from their hinges.

The place was dark and dreary and smelled of smoke, spilled liquor, and hot Mexican food. In one corner were grouped three or four men. One stood at the bar. And Ches lay sprawled on the floor in front of the bar, his gun still in its holster.

Drunk! He'd probably been too drunk to fight, too

drunk even to draw his gun. Mark's glance was furious, deadly, as it touched the bartender, standing shocked and motionless behind the shabby, ornate bar. It touched the man in front of the bar and blazed with fury.

The man had red hair and a deeply seamed face. He was scrawny and middle-aged. In the dim light, in this first quick glance, the man looked like Smead.

But it wasn't Smead. It was Red, the man over whose head Ches had broken the whisky bottle half a year before in Dawson's saloon down on the border.

Mark felt his body tense. Spread-legged, his arms hanging stiffly at his sides, he fought the haze of rage that drifted over his mind. He wanted to kill. It was like a hunger in him, an insatiable appetite.

He held onto himself desperately. He looked again at the bartender, holding Red in the corner of his eye. He asked flatly, "Fair fight?"

"Fair fight?" The bartender's fat face was incredulous. "Ches was so goddam drunk he didn't even get his hands off the bar. If he had, he'd have fallen down!"

Red whirled on him. "You lyin' son of a bitch! I ought to . . ."

Mark said, "Try it. Go ahead. Try it!"

Red swung his head. His forehead was shiny with sweat. He began frantically, "He . . ."

Mark raged, "He what?"

"He was goin' to kill me! I could tell. He tried to kill me once before down on the Mexican border."

Mark could see that Red did not recognize him. He'd grown, and filled out, and his clothes were different. When Red had last seen him he'd been a boy, swamping in a saloon. Now he was a man, holding a man's job.

His voice was level, deadly. He said deliberately, "Red, you're a lyin', yellow, crawlin' bastard! Now draw your gun. Let's see how good you are against a man that's sober."

Red didn't move, except to wipe his forehead with the hairy back of a trembling hand.

The hunger to kill crawled again in Mark's brain. He felt that old sensation of lightheadedness, of trembling nerves. A moral question, Ches had said. You had to make up your mind before you ever touched your gun. And Mark's mind was made up.

Mark said, "One way or another, I'm going to kill you. I'll count three and you'd better draw, because I will."

Red's eyes narrowed as he squinted at Mark. No recognition touched his face, though there was a puzzled frown on his brow.

Mark said softly, "Remember the kid you tried to hooraw in Dawson's down in Arizona?"

"You're him?" Red's voice was incredulous.

"I'm him." Tension was on the increase in Mark, becoming almost intolerable. He said tightly, "One . . ."

Red shifted his feet. His scared eyes shot to the bartender, then to the men across the room. They stared back at him with cold dislike.

"Two . . ."

He knew, then, that Red would draw. Red's mouth pinched down and his eyes grew flat, like a cornered animal's, staring at death, knowing that only a desperate fight would save him.

Mark opened his mouth for the third count but the word was never uttered. Red's body tensed and his hand shot wildly toward the grip of his gun. His action gave Mark an insight into his character he could have gotten no other way. Red was a man who gave himself, always, an advantage. Whether his opponent was a swamper in a saloon not yet out of his boyhood, a drunk who could scarcely see, or a man equal or better than he, he still had to give himself this edge.

Mark stared at him, willing his own body to react. He seemed to be locked and frozen to the floor. It was like a dream in which disaster leaps at you and you cannot move.

Then he felt the hard, cold grips of his gun against his palm. He felt the weight of the Colt's and felt it rise.

Amazement touched him briefly as he understood that he reacted automatically; training had taken over from a numbed, shocked mind.

The gun bucked against his palm before Red's was even level. The muzzle raised with recoil, snapped back into line, and the gun bucked again. Mark's second shot and Red's first blended into a single bark. Smoked filled the space between them, momentarily obscuring Red from Mark's sight.

Nothing moved but the drifting smoke, neither Red, hanging as though suspended on the bar's edge, nor Mark, nor the others in the room. Then Red's gun slipped from his fingers and clattered on the floor. Two spots of blood appeared on Red's shirt front. A man's hand could have covered them both.

Red's head slumped forward. His knees wobbled like rubber. All that held him up was his own weight bearing against the bar.

Mark's face grew pale. He wanted to empty his gun into Red's dead, upright body. His hands began to shake.

At last, Red buckled. He folded forward quietly, almost as though in relief. He hit the floor with a dull thump.

Mark holstered his gun. He stepped over and looked down at Ches. His eyes burned and his throat felt tight. "Look after him, kid," Clark had said. Damn!

Scowling, he knelt and laid his head against Ewing's chest. He heard no heartbeat. He picked up Ches's wrist—there was no pulse.

He looked helplessly at the fat, sweating bartender. "Where can I take him?"

The man hurried from behind the bar. "Come on, I'll show you."

Mark picked Ches up gently. Carrying him in his arms, he walked out the door into the warm evening dusk. Dumbly he followed along the street. He felt dead, unreal, like a sleepwalker. The tears he had blinked back before now welled from his eyes and ran across his cheeks.

A strange obsession was growing in his mind, and pain was like a twisting knife in his chest. Everyone he loved met a violent end—his mother, his father, Jaime, Rosa María. And now Ches—now Ches.

The undertaking parlor consisted of a small, bare room off the main room of the mercantile store. Mark carried Ches's body in and laid it gently on a long, narrow table. For a few moments he stood looking down at Ches's face.

Mark felt lost and alone as he turned away and went. outside.

The sheriff was waiting for him on the walk, a squat, powerful man with a face that betrayed to Mark both his distaste and his dislike. He said flatly, "I talked to the witnesses and it looks like you're in the clear. They say you didn't touch your gun until after Smead began his draw. But, by God, you forced the fight. Why couldn't you have let the law . . ."

Mark interrupted breathlessly, "Did you say Smead?"

The sheriff looked at him oddly. "Yeah. Smead. That was his name. Leastways there was a couple of letters on him addressed to Red Smead."

"Could I see them?" Mark's voice was unsteady.

The sheriff hesitated, studying Mark with sharp, unfriendly eyes. "Why? You didn't know him."

Mark said, trying to keep his voice even, "I knew

someone that looked like him. Someone named Sam Smead."

The sheriff shrugged. At last he took two crumpled envelopes from the pocket of his shirt. "Don't know what harm it could do."

Mark examined the envelopes. They were post-marked Denver, but bore no return address. Mark took a letter from one of the envelopes and looked at the signature. His heart thumped wildly in his chest. The letter was signed, "Sam."

Elation flushed his face. The date on the letter was June 29th, which meant that Sam Smead had been in Denver less than a month ago. He said, "Mind if I keep these?"

The sheriff hesitated, and while he did, Mark read the letter. It contained nothing of importance, and was simply an inquiry as to how his brother was. He read the other, too, which was dated March 12th, and also postmarked Denver. This one informed his brother that he had just arrived in Denver, and gave a brief description of the place.

The sheriff was still hesitating, eying the tied-down gun at Mark's thigh. "Somethin' tells me I hadn't ought to let you go. Who the hell are you, anyway? What're you after? It's hard to believe that a kid like you could get two bullets out of your gun while Smead was only getting off one. Hell, you ain't no more'n eighteen or nineteen."

Mark didn't answer. His mind was remembering Smead and Corbin and Healy, and what they'd done.

It was plain now why Red had reminded him of Smead.

But he couldn't let the sheriff hold him—not now, not if an explanation would keep him free. He said soberly, "Sheriff, when I was twelve, the Apaches killed my folks. I was taken in by a Mexican family named Ortega. They were killed when I was fourteen by three American scalp hunters who had discovered that you can't tell a Mexican scalp from that of an Apache. One of the scalp hunters was Sam Smead, the one that signed this letter."

The sheriff studied him doubtfully. "There's laws to take care of men like that."

Mark laughed sourly. "Laws! It happened more than four years ago, and they're still free. You're the law here, Sheriff. Suppose I turned it over to you? Would you leave here and track these scalpers down?"

"Well . . ."

"No, by God, you wouldn't. You couldn't. The crime was committed in Mexico. All the witnesses are down there. By the time you cut through all the difficulties, even if you could . . . Well, they'd get clear away. They'd go free, wouldn't they?"

The sheriff was silent, but Mark insisted harshly, "Wouldn't they?"

The sheriff nodded reluctantly. "Probably."

"Then you know why I'm taking it on myself. I've been practicing with this gun since I was fifteen so that when I came up with them I could do the job."

85

The sheriff shrugged. "All right, take the damn letters. An' I ain't sayin' I'm blamin' you for what you want to do. Only you get the hell out of Rio Blanco before somebody gets the notion to find out if you're as fast as them witnesses in the saloon said you were. You can bury your friend in the morning and right afterward you ride. Understand? I've got to keep the peace around here, an' it's liable to be tough with you in town."

Mark nodded. Turning, he headed for the two-story frame hotel. He got a room, went up to it, and locked the door behind him. He laid down wearily on the bed.

He wished Ches were here. Ches would have been as pleased as Mark was about this. A nervous, excited feeling ran through Mark's body. He had a trail! He had a trail at last!

He slept fitfully. Dozing, he dreamed of the stagecoach attack and of Healy and Corbin and Smead dumping their sacks of grisly trophies on Jaime Ortega's gallery floor. He could hear Healy laugh, almost as though the man were here in the room, with him.

He awoke, sweating. He got up, rolled a cigarette and smoked it. Then he sat at the window and stared down at the silent, sleeping town. Smead would lead him to Corbin, and Corbin would lead him to Healy.

Dawn streaked the eastern sky. Mark went downstairs and found a restaurant, where he drank three cups of black coffee. Then he walked to the mercantile store and made arrangements for Ches's funeral. The man that operated the store and the funeral parlor gave him the things that had been in Ches's pockets, and his gun and belt. Mark stowed the things in his saddlebags, not liking the memories they brought back to him.

He waited, then, squatting against the wall, watching the sun rise, smoking endless cigarettes. When the storekeeper called him, he went inside and helped carry Ches's casket out to the black hearse.

Then he rode behind with the sheriff as the hearse wound out of town and up onto the bare hill behind it where the cemetery was.

Arriving at the weed-grown cemetery, Mark and the sheriff helped unload the casket. There were two freshly dug graves here, side by side. One for the killer; one for the killed.

The undertaker said apologetically, "We ain't got no regular preacher hereabouts, but I'll read if you want."

Mark nodded briefly in appreciation. "I never heard him talk about religion, but I reckon he had some in him somewhere."

The man read in a solemn, sonorous voice while the early morning sun beat down upon the backs of Mark and the sheriff. And Mark was reminded of another funeral, when Jaime Ortega had read in Spanish and afterward, for Mark's benefit, had said in English, "The Lord giveth and the Lord taketh away. Blessed be the name of the Lord."

The man finished reading and closed his worn, leather-covered Bible. By using ropes, the three lowered the casket into the grave. Mark said, "I'd like to fill it in."

"Sure." The man gave Mark a shovel.

He worked steadily for about fifteen minutes, glad of the physical exertion, which somehow dulled his grief.

When he had finished, he tossed the shovel into the back of the hearse and mounted his horse. It would be different, now, and lonely. He wondered if his whole life would be as lonely as it now was.

He had an odd, somber feeling that somewhere along the trail ahead there were more graves and more plain pine boxes, one of them for Mark himself. He shook his head with angry impatience.

The undertaker spoke. "I'll put up a nice marker for him, son. Altogether it comes to twenty dollars."

Mark gave him a gold eagle. Then he rode back toward town beside the sheriff.

He went to the livery barn where Ches's horse had been taken, and traded Ches's saddle for a pack-saddle. Then, trailing Ches's horse, he rode back to the store and bought supplies to fill the panniers— enough supplies to last him all the way to Denver.

Chapter 8

FOR the next several days, Mark's own impatience was his greatest handicap. It made him want to ride day and night. It made him want to push his horses beyond the limits of their strength. All he could think about was Smead, and the incredible coincidence that had put him on Smead's trail. He was desperately afraid that when he did reach Denver, Smead would be gone without leaving a trace.

But Mark deliberately slowed himself to save his horses. The land was hot and dry as bone. The mountainous country through which he traveled necessitated many detours around the higher peaks.

In Taos, he lost half a day while a Spanish blacksmith shod his horses. But he stifled his impatience, and when the smith was done, rode on, reminded strongly of San Pablo as he passed the sleepy plaza, reminded again of the urgency of his journey and of the satisfaction that lay at its end.

Forty—fifty miles a day of the roughest kind of riding. At night, when he camped, he spent the first hour practicing his draw. How good Smead would be, he couldn't tell. But he didn't intend to lose; he couldn't lose. Beyond Smead there was Corbin, and Healy, who had led the band. Healy was the one Mark wanted most. Perhaps it was because Healy had so shocked him in San Pablo by his callous and offhand dumping of scalps on Jaime's gallery floor.

The mountains gave way to rolling plains, and then to mountains again. He struck a road at their foot and followed it. At last, descending the other side, he came into Colorado, and now the traveling was much easier, for the land stretched away, nearly flat, for as far as the eye could see.

He crossed the Arkansas, and there encountered a small party of Cheyenne braves. They eyed his horses with high interest, and when he had passed, fell in behind, talking among themselves excitedly.

Sight of them brought back to Mark his memories of Apaches. Their presence behind him made his nerves draw tight. Plainly they were after his horses and expected him to run. When he did, they would pursue, the very fact of his flight raising their confidence to the necessary pitch.

So, instead of running, he reined around, and, letting his pack horse go, galloped toward them.

They hauled up in surprise. Mark could see, as he drew near, that most of them were no older than he. They wore no paint. Probably a hunting party, but they apparently were not averse to stealing a couple of horses and guns if the cost were small. He had better show them that the cost would not be small.

They stood their ground until Mark was little more than a hundred yards away. A few of them reached for arrows to fit to their bows.

Five in all. Mark drew his Colt's swiftly and laid five bullets in the dust at their feet. The bullets all struck within a three-foot circle. Reaching into his saddlebags, Mark withdrew Ches's gun and laid a single shot over the Indians' heads.

It was enough. They turned their horses and fled.

Mark reined up, grinning, surprised that there was no hate in him for Indians any more. Time had mellowed his hatred. Would time mellow the hatred he bore for the scalpers?

Angrily he put the thought from him. Time would never still the hate he bore for Healy, for Corbin and Smead. Only death could still that hate. After all, he had no more reason to hate that party of young Cheyennes than he had to hate all Americans because three of them had killed his foster parents. Reassured, he put his mind to the trail ahead. . . .

Three days later he rode into the booming, brawling town of Denver.

Its size appalled him. He had never seen a town as large as this. Riding down its rutted, dusty streets, he gawked up at the two and three-story buildings, many of which were built with brick, and wondered how one man could find another in a city of this size.

He stared at the women, with their fancy gowns and ridiculous parasols. He stared at the gleaming carriages pulled by high-stepping horses and at the men, so important and prosperous-looking in their broadcloth suits. He fingered his soft beard, and looked down with distaste at his own dirty and trail-worn clothes.

Then he saw another segment of Denver's population—men like himself, roughly dressed, with guns at their thighs and rifles in their hands—and he felt better.

He stabled his horse at a place near Cherry Creek, and afterward walked the town tirelessly, searching without plan for the face of Sam Smead in the crowd.

All that evening he walked, and all the next day and all the next evening. But he did not find Smead.

In the morning, discouraged, he sat on the creaking bed in his hotel and dumped his leather money poke out on the covers. He stared at the small handful of coins in dismay. It cost money to live in a city. If he didn't find Smead soon . . .

He counted the coins. By careful management, he could last another week or more, but not over two. Then, he'd have to sell his pack horse and pack saddle. If necessary he'd sell his own horse. He wasn't going to let Smead go simply because he couldn't find him right away.

He ought to have a plan. There must be some way that a man could find another, even in a town as large as this.

He took out the letters and re-read them carefully, looking for some clue. There was none. But suddenly, as he was about to replace them in his pocket, his face lighted and he began to grin. The post office! Why hadn't he thought of that? If anyone in town could put him onto Smead, the postmaster could.

He left his room immediately. At the hotel desk, he inquired as to the location of the post office. Going out he hurried toward it.

He waited in line for a chance to talk to the man behind the barred window. The man was small, bald, and wore a green eyeshade and gold-rimmed spectacles.

Mark stepped up to the window, suddenly so overcome with anticipation that he could hardly talk. He showed the letters to the postmaster. "I'm looking for Sam Smead. His brother, the one he wrote these letters to, is dead."

And soon Sam Smead would be dead too, he thought. Soon.

The postmaster frowned as he searched his memory. "What kind of a lookin' man was he?"

Mark said, "About forty-five or fifty. Skinny man with deep wrinkles in his face. Reddish hair." Just remembering Smead, the way he looked, made Mark's heart beat fast, made tension and fury mount in his body.

The postmaster said, "Yeah. I think I do remember him. If it's the same one, he's a freighter, workin' between here and the gold camps in the mountains. I hold his mail for him and he picks it up. Don't know where he lives. You'll have to look around. But try the corrals and freightyards first. It's your best bet."

Mark thanked him earnestly. He left, feeling more hope than he'd felt since his arrival.

He got his horse and began to make the rounds of the corrals and freightyards. At the fifth one, he learned that Smead was now at a new gold camp in the mountains, known as Gregory Gulch.

Mounting, Mark rode out, heading west. He splashed across the Platte and crossed the grassy plain along the heavily traveled wagon road. Looking back, he could see an Indian village nestling close to the western edge of the town.

It was now late August, and the days were blistering hot. But when he reached the mountains, it cooled perceptibly. By night, it was chilly enough for a fire and two blankets.

He encountered a line of wagons returning toward Denver early the next morning while still several miles short of Gregory Gulch. He pulled aside to let them pass, searching the face of every driver in the line . . .

His heart jumped—Smead was driving the last wagon. Mark pulled into the middle of the road and stopped his horse.

Staring at the hated features of Smead, he could feel his face flushing. The old sensation of lightheadedness came back, the old feeling that every nerve in his body was jumping and twitching.

Smead cracked his whip out over the backs of his teams. He yelled, "Get outa the goddam road! What the hell's the matter with you?"

Mark held his ground. More than anything in the world he wanted to kill Smead now. He wanted to force Smead to stop. He wanted to tell Smead who he was. He wanted to see the look on Smead's face when he told him he'd come from San Pablo to avenge the deaths of Jaime Ortega and Rosa María.

But he knew he could not. If he shot Smead, half a dozen rifles would bring him down before he could reach cover on the mountainside. The other drivers would not hear his words. They would see but one thing, a stranger shooting down their employer for no apparent reason.

Mark moved out of the road at the last minute. The intensity of his stare brought a flush of anger to Smead's gaunt, deeply seamed face. Smead tried to stare back, but in the end dropped his glance and ostentatiously turned his attention to his driving.

Mark fell in behind, traveling just far enough back to be out of the dust. He grinned bleakly when Smead swung his head to look around.

Smead looked back many times during the rest of the day. And each time he did, Mark grinned wickedly. Let him sweat, he thought. Let him worry. Let him wonder, "What have I done to this one? Where is this one from?"

At dusk, Mark pulled away and climbed the hillside. He camped in a grove of trees out of sight of the teamsters below. But in the morning, when they pulled out at dawn, he was there, just a little behind them.

The day dragged along. At first, Smead swung his head often on his scrawny neck to look behind. Then, for a while, he kept his glance determinedly straight ahead. But he couldn't stick it out. He had to look again and see if Mark was there.

The wagons crossed the Platte and entered Denver.

They wound through the streets until they reached a corral on the western edge of town. Mark reined up outside.

The sun dropping in the west. The high-piled clouds above the eastern plain glowed rose and gold, like clouds above the desert. Memory came flooding back to Mark, memory that made him shiver imperceptibly.

He saw Smead stride from the corral by an alley gate. He galloped around to intercept him when he left the alley. There, in the middle of the alley, he sat his horse and watched Smead walk uncertainly toward him.

A dozen yards away, Smead halted. His hand moved toward the gun at his hip, then stopped and dangled at his side. He called blusteringly, "Whaddaya want? What the hell you followin' me for?"

Mark swung off his fidgeting horse. He stood solidly in the middle of the alley. He said, "I'm going to kill you."

"Kill me?" There was a touch of panic in Smead's voice. "For God's sake, what for? I've never seen you before in my life!"

"Yes you have. Want me to tell you where? San Pablo."

Smead jerked as though he had been shot. His right arm tensed like a claw, but made no move toward his gun.

Mark said, "Want to tell me where to find Corbin and Healy?"

"You got the wrong man, mister. I don't know nobody by them names."

"Liar!" He began to pace steadily toward Smead. "Want to know how I found you after all these years? Pure luck. Your brother killed a friend of mine and I took it up and killed your brother. I found these letters on his body."

He tossed the letters at Smead's feet. His mouth twisted. Suddenly he seemed to be smelling the sweetish, wild odor of the Apache scalps that Healy had dumped out on the gallery floor so long ago in San Pablo.

He said furiously, "God damn you, pull your gun! Or would you rather I beat you to death with mine?"

Smead seemed to wilt. "What if I give you a line on Corbin an' Healy? Hell, Healy's the one you want. He was the boss. It was his idea."

"Where are they?"

"You'll let me alone if I tell you?"

Mark shook his head. Hate choked him and made his stomach churn.

Smead blurted, "I got letters from them in my room. They're a couple of years old, but they'll be a lead."

Mark's nausea increased. Smead had no loyalty even to his friends. He said, "All right. We'll get the letters. It'll buy you an hour, but that's all."

He watched Smead's face and saw slyness creep into it. He knew Smead might well lead him into some kind of trap, but it was a chance he'd have to take.

Smead sidled past him cautiously and walked up the street. Mark followed, leading his horse.

Smead stopped at an outside stairway leading up over a saddlery store. Mark tied his horse to the rail watchfully, then followed Smead up the stairway. He stayed back far enough to be out of reach of Smead's feet, should the man turn and kick at him.

Smead unlocked the door and entered, and Mark stepped quickly to the landing behind him. Smead tried to slam the door, but Mark stuck a foot into it, and lunged against it.

It gave, and Mark crashed into Smead in the dark hallway. Smead went rolling to the floor, and Mark, off balance, went to his knees.

In the blinding darkness, Mark laid a shot down the hallway. Smead screeched, "No! Don't do that! For God's sake!"

Mark got up cautiously. Smead's form was a blur as the scalper got to his feet. Mark said harshly, "Strike a match and light a lamp. One more stunt like that will be your last!"

A match flared in Smead's hand. His face was white as chalk. He led the way through a door and touched the match to the wick of a coal-oil lamp. He lowered the chimney and light filled the room.

Mark's eyes clung to the lamp a second too long. He felt a burning sensation along his ribs, like the cut of a whip, and instantly thereafter heard the bellow of Smead's gun. Acrid powdersmoke billowed toward him.

He flung himself aside instinctively just as Smead's gun roared again. He felt his own gun grips in his hand, felt his thumb against the curving surface of the hammer. Through the cloud of powdersmoke, Smead was a blurred, crouching figure.

Mark's gun muzzle centered with automatic precision and the gun bucked in his hand, centered, and bucked again.

Smead, was flung against the wall as though struck by a fist. The building creaked with the impact. Then Smead slid down the wall to a sitting position and stayed there, his eyes wide, but dead and without expression. His mouth fell open and hung slackly.

Mark stared at him for a moment, feeling none of the exhilaration he should have felt. The nausea that had started earlier, now came back.

He swallowed, gritted his teeth and turned away. He went into the hall and to the door at its end. He opened it slightly and listened for a full two minutes. Save for the normal noises in the street, he heard nothing.

His body felt cold as he returned to Smead's room. Smead still sat against the wall, as though resting. His head lolled to one side, but his eyes remained open, staring at nothing.

Mark shuddered slightly and began to rummage through the papers in Smead's roll-top desk.

The letters were in a cubbyhole, hidden behind a wadded rag. Mark pulled them out and carried them over to the lamp. He leafed through them quickly.

He was not able to identify the ones he wanted by the envelopes, so he sat down and began to pull them, one by one, from the envelopes and look at the signatures.

And there, at the bottom, he found the two he sought. One was signed Abe and postmarked Chimney Rock, New Mexico. The other was signed Greco and postmarked Abilene.

Mark stuffed them into his pocket and left without a backward glance.

Now he had to decide which of the two he wanted first. Healy was the most dangerous, he knew, so he'd go after Corbin first, and if Healy got him before he got Healy, at least Corbin and Smead would be out of the way.

He returned to his room and laid down, fully clothed, on the bed. Tomorrow, the hue and cry would begin. Smead's body would be found and his teamsters would remember Mark as the one who had followed them so tenaciously from the mountains.

So he had to leave, and soon. He got up and went downstairs into the street. Wandering aimlessly along, he noticed wires strung between poles overhead. The telegraph! Why hadn't he thought of it before? He could wire Abilene and find out if Corbin was there. He might, in this way, save himself a month of riding, might get to Healy sooner.

He inquired as to the location of the telegraph office, and went there at once. A man with a green eyeshade took his message and began to clack his key: MARSHAL, ABILENE, KANSAS. GRECO CORBIN, LAST REPORTED ABILENE, WANTED HERE FOR MURDER. ADVISE HIS PRESENT LOCATION. Mark signed the telegram ATKINS, DENVER, certain that the Abilene marshal would assume he was an officer of the law.

Then he sat down to wait.

The hours passed. Messages came in and went out over the swiftly clacking instrument. The operator did not look up at Mark.

There had been a reason for Mark's wording his telegraph message in the way he had. He doubted if the marshal in Abilene would bother to answer a message from a citizen with no cloak of authority. And yet, he had committed no deception for which he could be successfully prosecuted.

He tried to remember Corbin, and found that he had nearly forgotten the man. He wondered what Corbin had done in the years between now and the murderous attack on San Pablo. Had he followed the trail of violence? Or had he settled in some honest business the way Smead had?

What if he had a wife—and children? Scowling, Mark shook his head. It would make no difference. Corbin must die, as Smead had—as Healy would.

Dawn streaked the sky outside. Freight wagons began to rumble through the streets. A drunk staggered past.

The sun came up and shone through the windows of the telegraph office. The operator blinked at Mark and adjusted the eyeshade against the glare.

Mark began to fidget. Maybe Abilene didn't intend to answer. Maybe . . .

The telegraph instrument clacked busily. The operator turned and handed Mark a slip of paper. "Here you are. Sounds like somebody saved you a trip to Abilene."

Mark read the message: ATKINS, DENVER MARSHAL. CORBIN KILLED THREE MONTHS AGO—GUNFIGHT—ABILENE. SORRY. It was signed, SMITH, MARSHAL'S OFFICE, ABILENE, KANSAS.

An odd, unexplainable feeling of relief ran through Mark. Getting up, he grinned slightly at the success of his ruse.

He walked to his hotel, wondering at this relief he felt, wondering at his lack of disappointment.

He gathered up his effects, paid his bill and left. He got his horse at the stable, and there sold the pack animal and pack saddle for sixty dollars. He rode out, heading south.

Smead was dead, and Corbin too. Now there was only Healy. Yet in spite of himself, Mark kept remembering the staring eyes of Smead as the man sagged against the wall of his tiny room. He remembered his own nausea and self-disgust.

A moral question a man has got to settle with himself before he touches his gun, Ches had said. Mark had settled the moral question long ago in his mind. He'd set out to kill the scalpers. But it seemed, suddenly, as though life had never held anything for Mark but vengeance, corroding and souring his soul, making impossible the human relationships that other men take for granted.

He camped, and slept, and rode on again. The land lay before him and around him, vast and nearly empty, gradually giving him peace from regret by its very immensity, by its very stillness.

Back over the mountains he went. Entering New Mexico, he turned west according to directions he'd received. At last, nearly two weeks after leaving Denver, he saw in the distance the towering red sandstone spire that marked the town of Chimney Rock. It rose above the surrounding plain like a varicolored castle in the fading sunlight, towering several hundred feet in the air.

Mark reined in, knowing in this instant that he stood at a crossroads. For the first time, he knew fear—not fear that he would be killed, but fear of a future that would hold no burning need for vengeance. With Healy dead, what would he do? Where would he go?

He began to wonder if Healy, like Corbin, were not already dead.

Conflicting desires worked back and forth through his mind. Remembering how he had felt after killing Smead, he almost hoped that Healy was already dead.

Troubled and confused, he let his horse lag as he rode toward town, dreading what he might find. At last, on its very outskirts, he knew what he wanted most. He wanted Healy to be gone, to have left no trace behind. With no trail to follow, he could forget, and begin to live a different life.

He was not proud of this desire; nor was he ashamed of it. He knew only that, regardless of his personal feelings, he was committed to go on until the job was done.

Chapter 9

CHIMNEY ROCK was not a large town. Most of the business buildings were located on the one main street, Center Street. The Alamo Hotel, an ornate frame building in need of paint, and the livery barn, at the foot of the street, dominated it. In the middle of Center Street, before the hotel, was a windmill and a concrete stock tank. The overflow made a sea of mud around the tank.

A couple of small boys were sailing a boat in the tank as Mark rode in. Somewhere a woman's voice called to them, and they scooted away, giving Mark a lingering appraisal.

He let his horse drink at the tank, his glance roving over the town and beyond, to the spire of rock that undoubtedly gave the town its name.

Then, wearily, he rode to the livery barn and swung down. The liveryman, nondescript and middle-aged, spat tobacco juice at the wall and said in a reedy voice, "Two bits a day for feedin' your horse. Includes grain."

Mark flipped him a quarter and the man caught it

expertly. He followed the man back into the stable. "Does a man named Abe Healy live here in Chimney Rock?"

The stableman laughed. "Did. Don't no more. Been gone a year or more. Hope he stays gone, too."

An odd relief settled on Mark. It angered him vaguely. Nobody was forcing him to hunt Healy—if he felt this way, why didn't he quit?

He said, "Know anybody that might know where he went?"

The stableman turned and peered at him in the semi-darkness. "Friend of his?"

"No. Just looking for him."

"That gal of his might know. Susan Kerby. Works in the hotel, cookin' an' waitin' tables. Ask her. Don't ask me."

Mark said, "Thanks," and turned away. The air was warm and the cottonwoods a block over on the residential street rustled in the breeze. A dog barked. There was a mingled smell of cedarwood smoke and frying meat in the air. A peaceful town, thought Mark. A pleasant one.

Against the graying sky to eastward, he saw the spire of a church, topped with a small cross.

He walked down the dusty street and crossed, skirting the mud around the windmill-fed tank. He entered the hotel, a three-story structure on the corner with a wide roofed veranda on two sides. There were two or three men on the veranda, their rocking chairs squeaking steadily, their cigars making spots of light against the semi-darkness.

The lobby floor was tiled. Its walls were hung with game heads: elk and deer, wolves and mountain lions. There were heavy dark-oak benches along the walls and in the center of the lobby, each equipped with a shiny brass spittoon.

Mark's heels clicked as he crossed to the oak desk. A bald, elderly man looked up, peering over the glasses that sat on his nose, and said, "Howdy, stranger. Want a room?"

Mark nodded, grinning faintly. The man shoved the register toward him and Mark signed, *Mark Atkins. San Pablo, Sonora.*

I'll leave that there, he thought. Some time after I'm gone, Healy might return. He might just happen to see that name and that town on the hotel register.

The man peered at Mark more closely. "Far from home, ain't you?"

Mark nodded. The man said, "Room's fifty cents. Take Twelve, at the top of the stairs. If you're stayin' a while, maybe I could make you a better rate."

Mark said, "I don't know if I am or not." He looked across at the entrance to the dining room. Then he climbed the stairs heavily.

He washed, shaved and combed his hair. Then he descended to the lobby again and crossed to the dining room.

It was almost as large as the lobby, and was also floored with tile. There were no more than half a dozen people eating. Mark selected a table and sat down, facing the door. He looked around for Susan Kerby.

Mark didn't know exactly what he'd expected. A woman with eyes that knew too much, perhaps—one with lines in her face and gray in her hair. So when a girl no more than seventeen or eighteen came from the kitchen and moved toward him, his mouth fell open with surprise.

She grinned boyishly at him as she came up to his table. "Haven't you ever seen a woman before?"

Mark flushed slightly, then grinned back. "Was it that noticeable?"

She nodded. "Stranger, aren't you?"

"Yes." He studied her closely, until she flushed. Noticing that, he dropped his glance.

She said, "Beef stew, roast beef or steak. Which will it be?"

"The stew."

He watched her move away, unbelieving. This couldn't be Susan Kerby. A girl like this wouldn't . . .

He frowned, trying to remember Healy. The man had possessed a kind of natural charm. Jaime had seen through it, Mark remembered, but Rosa María hadn't.

Susan was a small girl, who wouldn't come higher than the point of Mark's shoulder. Her hair was a rich dark brown, drawn back away from her face and put up in a mass of curls at the back of her neck. Her skin reminded Mark of the white petals of the prairie sand lily, and her eyes were dark and warm.

She walked with an easy, natural grace that fascinated him, reminding him of a doe in a mountain park.

Healy's woman! Mark tore his eyes from her and stared at the table before him. Anger stirred in his mind.

He lifted his eyes to Susan Kerby again, and knew suddenly that she wasn't Healy's woman. Not yet. No woman that belonged to Healy could fail to show the marks of it. And Susan did not.

She brought his food and placed the dishes on the table before him. Her color was high and her eyes avoided his. For some reason, this pleased him.

When she had left, he examined his own mind carefully. He'd had no experience with women. He didn't need it to know that Susan Kerby had held an instant and immediate attraction for him. Nor to guess that she liked him as well.

He smiled to himself as he ate. It was pleasant, being liked, particularly by a pretty woman like Susan. He caught himself watching her as she moved about the dining room. He discovered a rising excitement within himself that had nothing to do with Healy. It was hunger to be loved, to forsake the lonely life that had been his for so long.

He frowned at some vague thought that crossed his mind, then put it away from him determinedly. But it lingered, hovering in the back of his thoughts.

He shook his head angrily. It was nonsense to believe that everyone he loved met a violent end. And yet, wasn't that exactly what had happened?

When he had finished, she came and gathered up his plates. "That will be twenty-five cents."

He laid a quarter on the table. An odd tension gripped him. He looked up and met her eyes. Their glances held. "How late do you work?" he asked.

"Till eight."

"If I wait on the veranda would you let me walk you home?"

"Yes." She did not hesitate, nor did she mask her eyes with coquettishness.

Mark grinned exuberantly. "I'll be there." He got up and walked out onto the veranda. The three men were still there, rocking and talking in low tones. Mark found himself a chair near the door. It was seven-thirty.

Sitting there, he realized that he had forgotten for a while why he wanted to see Susan Kerby. He had forgotten Healy and the vengeance trail altogether. Remembering it now put a sour taste in his mouth.

Deliberately he forced himself to remember Jaime Ortega and Rosa María, whose lives Healy had taken for less than a hundred pesos that he hadn't even collected. He let himself realize there could be no future for him, with Susan Kerby or with any other woman, until Healy was dead.

But he didn't leave. His eyes kept seeing the way she walked across the tiled dining-room floor. He kept recalling the steady warmth of her eyes, the full promise of her mouth.

Excitement coursed through him and his mind

indulged in the universal fantasies of youth. He could almost feel her warmth against him, could almost taste the sweetness of her mouth.

He smiled ruefully in the darkness. This, after seeing the girl once. This, when he didn't know a thing about her except that she knew Abe Healy.

A heavy step on the veranda stairs roused him. He glanced up, and his eyes caught a glint of metal against the newcomer's vest. "Evenin'," the sheriff said.

Mark nodded.

"New in town, ain't you?"

"That's right."

"Stayin'?"

"I don't know."

"Mind stepping into the lobby a minute?"

Mark got up and followed the sheriff into the lobby. Tenseness came into his body.

The sheriff looked at him closely. "Been up towards Denver lately?"

"Why?"

"There's a description out on a killer that might fit you. Came in this mornin'."

The old lightheadedness came over Mark. But he forced a grin to his mouth. "My description could fit a hundred men."

"That's right, it. could." The sheriff studied his eyes as though trying to read his mind. At last he said, "Son, from where I stand, you look like trouble. I don't give a damn what happened up in Denver. As long as I don't *know* you're the man they want, well, I'll let it go. But I do care what happens in Chimney Rock. Keep it in mind. Start trouble in my town—"

He broke off suddenly. So intent had he been upon Mark that he had not heard the approach of Susan Kerby. "Hello, Sheriff," she said.

The sheriff swung toward her, then looked suspiciously back at Mark. "Remember, son. Any kind of trouble—any kind at all."

Mark didn't miss the implication. He felt himself flushing with anger.

Susan eased the tension with her smiling, "Don't look so grim, Sheriff."

"Was I looking grim? Sorry." But the sheriff's eyes still held Mark's, hard and cold and filled with warning. He said, "This is a fine girl. I have an idea I'd make plenty of trouble for any man that hurt her."

Mark said, "Wouldn't blame you." He looked at Susan. "Shall we go?"

"Yes."

Mark held the door for her awkwardly and followed her out. She paused for a moment on the walk and pulled her shawl closer around her shoulders. She breathed deeply, her head thrown back, and looked at the sky. Mark said, "My name's Mark—Mark Atkins."

"I'm Susan Kerby. What was all that about back there in the lobby?"

Mark said, "The sheriff was doing his job, that's all. A friendly warning not to start trouble."

He stood close beside her, feeling her nearness, feeling an unaccustomed pleasure because of it. He groped for words to say, but found none. The silence grew awkward. Mark began to fidget with embarrassment.

Suddenly Susan laughed. It was a pleasant sound. She said, "Aren't we the talkative ones?"

Mark chuckled. "I'm not used to girls—can't think of things to say. Which way do you live?"

"This way." She took his arm in a firm grip and turned him around. They moved slowly along the walk, with Mark acutely conscious of her hand on his arm.

He said, "Nice town," and grinned inwardly at the obviousness of his remark. Next thing he knew he'd be talking about the weather. He suddenly envied men he had seen who could talk easily with pretty women.

Susan said, "It is a nice town. I like it. Are you planning to stay?"

He shrugged without answering. He realized suddenly how desperately he wanted to stay. "Are the ranches hereabouts hiring?"

"I doubt it. Most of them have probably hired their roundup help."

He wanted to ask her about Healy—the question was fairly shouting in his mind. But he didn't know how to put it without spoiling this startling closeness that had sprung up between them.

"Where are you from, Mr. Atkins?" Her voice was

low, and possessed a quality that in itself stirred him.

"Sonora. A Mexican family named Ortega raised me." That wasn't strictly true, but it would do. Maybe it would also lead him into his question about Healy. He said, "Come to think of it, a man from here visited with them once. Name of Healy. Abe Healy. Do you know him?"

She brightened immediately. "Of course I know Abe. He's one of my closest friends. In fact . . ." She stopped.

"In fact what?"

"He has asked me to marry him. But . . . well, I haven't decided."

Anger flooded Mark. His head echoed with it. Healy and Susan Kerby! Marriage! It was unthinkable!

Susan stopped abruptly. When she spoke, there was a touch of fear in her voice. "What's the matter, Mr. Atkins?"

"Matter? Nothing's the matter."

"Oh, but it is. You forget, my hand was on your arm. A person doesn't tighten up like you did over nothing."

Mark's mind raced. He knew he couldn't tell her now. She'd never believe such a story from a man she'd known less than two hours. And he realized suddenly that he couldn't bear either her anger or her scorn.

He said quickly, "He's so much older than you."

Susan laughed, with uneasy relief. "Not so awfully much. I'm almost eighteen. He's not more than twenty-seven or twenty-eight."

Mark said, "He's a fool."

"Why do you say that?" Her eyes studied him in the faint light of the stars.

"He'd have to be a fool to go off and leave you. I wouldn't, if I were Healy."

She laughed with relief, and made a mock curtsey. "A pretty speech, Mr. Atkins," she said teasingly.

Her face made an oval blur in the darkness. Excitement coursed through Mark as he stared down at her.

Her eyes were wide, her lips parted slightly. She seemed like a bird, half frightened, half fascinated. Her words and her laugh had been too nervous, serving only to hide her fright.

Mark said, "Susan . . ."

"I've got to get home, Mr. Atkins." Fright was plain in her voice.

"All right." He looked down into her soft, shining eyes. He wanted to seize her in his arms, but he knew it was too soon.

He groped for, and found, her hand. Then he turned and went on, slowly, down the street.

She walked silently beside him. He wondered if she had felt back there the things that he had felt. His heart thumped almost audibly in his chest.

They reached her house and stopped outside the white picket gate. Susan said, "You'll be leaving soon, won't you? When?"

Mark hesitated a moment, then said, "Not for a while. Maybe I could find a job. Maybe one of the ranches . . ." He wished he could tell her the things he felt for her. He said, "I want to see you again."

"All right."

An odd kind of strain was between them suddenly. Susan laughed nervously. Then she gently disengaged her hand, which he still held, turned and went through the gate. With the gate between them, she smiled at him. "Good night, Mark."

"Good night. I'll see you tomorrow."

"Yes." She ran up the walk toward the house.

Mark watched until the door had closed behind her. Then he headed down the street toward the hotel, marveling at the feelings that had been born in him these last two hours.

His mind returned to Healy, and for the first time in years, he could remember Healy, the way he had looked, the way he had talked. His mind created an image of Healy, big, wild, smelling of sage and smoke and campfire grease, holding Susan Kerby in his arms.

A chill of revulsion ran along Mark's spine, the same sort of chill a man might feel upon encountering a scorpion in his boot.

Uneasiness mingled with the rising anger in him. It couldn't be. And yet, how could Mark stop it? He didn't dare become involved with Susan himself. She was Healy's girl. And besides . . .

He thought of his parents, of the Ortegas, of Ches Ewing. No. He didn't dare love Susan Kerby. Yet he also knew it was too late—he already loved her, incredible as it seemed. He was caught. He couldn't help himself.

Chapter 10

MARK saw Susan every day, several times a day, during the next few days. He ate all his meals at the hotel, timing them so that most of the other diners would be gone and Susan would have a moment to sit with him over a lingering cup of coffee. Each night, he met her outside the hotel when she got off at eight o'clock, and walked her home in the warm night air.

For the first time in his life, something moved in to push the thirst for vengeance out of his mind. His thoughts dwelt on Susan exclusively. He forgot Healy, the Ortegas, Ches Ewing, everything but this girl, who made his blood pound when he was with her, who made him miserable when he was not.

A week after his arrival, walking toward her house, he changed direction deliberately, and walked her instead to the edge of town, where willows grew along the narrow creek, where the moon was bright, illuminating the towering spire of Chimney Rock like a monstrous monument.

They sat in the warm grass, listening to the crickets chirp, listening to a frog croaking somewhere at the edge of the creek.

Susan was oddly silent. She lay back on the grass and clasped her hands behind her head. She stared up at the starry sky. "It's a beautiful night, isn't it, Mark?"

He turned toward her. He had never seen anything

quite as beautiful as her face in moonlight. He said, "You're beautiful."

"Mark, please . . . You're going away. Don't say things you're going to be sorry for."

Mark turned on his side and looked down into her face. He saw fright in her eyes, but he saw a need, too, the same need that burned so fiercely within himself.

He put a hand gently on the side of her face and turned it toward him. Under his hand, a fast pulse beat in her throat. Her lips parted, and her breath was sweet and warm in his nostrils. His arms went hungrily around her. His lips found hers.

For a moment she struggled, her body tense. Then the tension left it. Her arms went tight around his neck.

Hunger and tenderness mingled in Mark like an acute pain. A savage, wonderful joy soared in his brain. The fire mounted in his heart.

Susan pulled away, struggling. "Mark! No!"

He kissed the hollow of her throat, feeling the rise and fall of her breasts beneath his chest. She said again, pleadingly, "Mark. No. Please."

He raised his head and looked down into her eyes. "I love you. Oh God, how I love you."

She was silent, her eyes searching his face with a kind of desperation. She seemed to be waiting for something.

Guilt entered Mark's mind, spoiling the beauty of the moment. And with the guilt, thoughts of Healy returned. He pulled away.

The fires of need died slowly, but he was glad they were dying. Another moment . . . another moment and it would have been too late.

He had to tell her—had to tell her why he was here, why he hunted Healy, and what Healy had done.

Inwardly he cursed himself, wondering where this unreasoning sense of honor had come from. Why could he not take this moment and treasure it and forget all else? Why did he feel that Susan must know before there could be anything real and good between them?

She would not believe him when he did tell her. She would think he had sought her out and made love to her only for the purpose of gaining her confidence so she would tell him where Healy had gone.

He got to his feet, reached down and helped Susan up. There was tension in her body, and a strange coldness about her face.

He put his hands on her shoulders. "I've thought of nothing but you since the first night I saw you." He pulled her to him and laid his face against her fragrant hair. Confusion boiled in his thoughts.

She lifted her face. "Something's the matter, Mark. What is it?"

"Not tonight,' he said, "Some other time."

"All right, Mark." The tension went out of her and she smiled.

With his arm around her waist, Mark walked her back to town. Along the quiet street they went, and stopped before the picket gate.

She stood on tiptoe and kissed him lightly on the mouth. Then she turned and went through the gate.

Mark did not return at once to the hotel. Instead he wandered back to the place beside the creek and stood there staring moodily at the water. . . .

He continued to see Susan during the days that followed, but it became progressively more difficult for him to tell her the things he knew he must eventually reveal.

Between times, while Susan worked, he rode the country side looking for a job that would keep him for the winter, that would make it possible for him to stay, but he had no success. Most of the ranches had their roundup help. A few that didn't offered him short-term jobs with the understanding that he would be laid off as soon as roundup was finished.

He knew he should have taken one of these, but his time with Susan was short and he couldn't bear to give up any of it.

He was in love with her, wildly and desperately. Healy and his vengeance were forgotten. Mark wanted nothing in the world but to stay here, find a job, and marry Susan.

Yet all the time, the strange obsession that had begun when Ches was killed, lingered in the back of his thoughts. At times, when he was feeling discouraged, reason strengthened it. Sooner or later, Healy had to return. And when he did—when he did, Mark knew the hatred he felt would have to erupt in violence.

September passed, and the wind blew cool from the high peaks in Colorado. At last, on a crisp October evening, sitting on the porch swing in front of Susan's boardinghouse, Mark plunged in with reckless desperation. "Where did Healy go, Susan? And when's he coming back?"

She looked at him strangely. "I don't know either of those things, Mark. He's a cattle trader. He goes away from Chimney Rock regularly on business. Sometimes he's gone a few weeks, but occasionally he's gone for months. I doubt if he himself knows when he'll be coming back."

Mark realized his hands were trembling. He was more scared than he'd ever been in his life before. But he knew he had to tell her—now. He said deliberately, "I told you that Healy had visited with the Ortegas down in Sonora, Susan, but I didn't tell you why. You don't know Abe Healy, Susan."

He felt her stiffen beside him, and rushed on, knowing that if he stopped now he'd never tell her. "Healy was a scalp hunter. He had two partners, one of them named Corbin, the other Smead. They hunted Apaches in northern Sonora and sold the scalps to the Mexican government. The night they stopped in San Pablo they had two sacks with thirty-seven Apache scalps in them—scalps of men, women, and children too."

Susan was silent, whether shocked or disbelieving, Mark couldn't tell. He hurried on tensely, "About a week after they passed through San Pablo, they came back. The government had cut the bounties in half, and Healy and his friends had got the notion they could get even. They attacked the village in the middle of the night. They killed nearly a dozen people before they were driven off. Do you know why, Susan? Because they'd discovered that you can't tell a Mexican scalp from that of an Apache. And Mexican scalps were a lot easier to take—or so they thought."

He was silent a moment. He did not look at Susan. He could feel his body turn cold as memory came flooding back. He shivered noticeably. Then he went on, his voice harsh with anger, "Among the dead were Jaime and Rosa María Ortega, who had picked me up after my folks were killed."

He turned his head and looked at Susan. In the soft glow from the window behind her, her face was bloodless. Her eyes were cold, her lips compressed. She said furiously, "I've never heard such a fantastic lie in my life! You must be insane! Why did you make up this crazy story? Why?"

Mark laughed bitterly. "I didn't make it up. But maybe I am insane—insane enough to have thought of nothing but catching and killing those three since the day it happened. Insane enough to have trained myself to use a gun every day for almost five years. Insane enough to have tracked Smead down and killed him." He laughed again. "And insane enough to find Healy and kill him too, by God!"

Susan stared at him in shocked disbelief. "Then

that's why . . . And I thought . . ." She got to her feet, standing small and straight, trembling. Her face was dead white, her eyes filled with hurt. When she spoke, her voice was icy, shaking. "Get away from me, Mark Atkins! I don't think I ever want to see you. You used me! You lied to me! You pretended . . ." She whirled, and started furiously toward the door.

Mark caught her. He turned her around savagely, gripping her arms until her face twisted with pain. "Listen to me! Damn it, listen! I looked you up in the hotel because the stableman said you knew Healy. But from the moment I saw you I forgot about him. Do you hear? I forgot about him. I fell in love with you."

"You lie! All you know is hate!"

"No, Susan. I couldn't lie about that. I love you. I swear to God!"

"Then why did you ask me where he had gone? Why did you tell me this horrible story?"

He said wearily, "Sit down and hear me out." He pulled her gently back toward the swing and she sat down stiffly. Her back was straight and defiant; her eyes stared straight ahead.

He said, "First it was my mother and father. They were killed by Apaches near Tucson when I was twelve. Jaime Ortega found me and took me to live with him in San Pablo. I loved Jaime and I loved Rosa María. They were good to me. But Healy and his friends killed them."

He halted. Susan hadn't moved, nor had her face softened. Mark went on, "I ran away from San Pablo and came north across the border alone. I knew I wasn't old enough, so I worked more than four years in a saloon down near the border, swamping. When I figured I was big enough, I left there with a man named Chester Ewing."

His voice softened with memory of those first days with Ches. "He was like a father to me—but he was killed too. Can't you see, Susan? Something seems to happen to everyone I love. I don't want anything to happen to you!"

"I don't see . . ."

Mark said patiently, "Healy is bound to come back."

Susan's body began to tremble violently. "And you are bound to kill him, is that it?"

"I don't know. I don't know! That's why I had to tell you."

She faced him furiously. "You don't know what love is, Mark. I'm glad I found it out in time. All you understand is hate. You used me. You made love to me just to make me trust you, to make me tell you where Abe went. Well, you wasted your time, because I don't know. And I wouldn't tell you if I did. You're crazy! You're all twisted up. Abe's not the man you want. He couldn't do what you've said he did. I know him." Her voice rose hysterically. "I tell you I know Abe! Maybe he isn't steady. But he isn't full of hate, either—not like you are. And he's not a murderer."

She seemed to seize on that in desperation. "How many have *you* killed besides this Smead? How many more will you kill before you're through? Oh God, I should have listened to the sheriff. He said there was something wrong with you. He said you were too cold—too good with your gun." She was sobbing so that she could hardly talk. Mark put out a hand and touched her arm. She shuddered and jerked it away as though a snake had crawled across it.

Mark got up angrily. "Maybe it wasn't what I thought it was between you and me. Seems to me you're mighty damn ready to say I'm wrong and Abe's right!"

She didn't reply. Mark felt sick inside. His brain felt numb and his vision blurred. But he could see the revulsion in her face and the terrible hurt in her eyes. He said wearily, "Why do you think I waited so long to tell you? I was afraid you'd take it this way. I was afraid you'd think I was lying about being in love with you, that you'd think I only wanted you to tell me where Healy was. But it isn't true!"

She didn't answer him. The sound of her sobs was like a knife turning in his chest. He said, "That night on the creekbank. I wanted to ask you to marry me then. But I couldn't—not until you knew. I couldn't . . ." He sighed. "Oh hell, what's the use?"

He waited a moment more, hoping that she would speak. When she didn't, he turned and went down the steps. Almost blindly, he stumbled along the street.

He stopped in front of the saloon and stared at it moodily. Was this why Ches had needed his liquor so? Had Ches needed to forget something like this that lay in his past?

Mark pushed his way through the swinging doors. He went to the bar and ordered a bottle and glass. Then he took them to a table and sat down heavily.

For a few moments he stared at the bottle and empty glass. He didn't want the liquor. But he did want to forget the sound of Susan's sobs. He wanted to forget the bitterness and hurt that had been in her voice.

He poured a drink and downed it. He made a wry face and immediately poured another. From another table, where he sat playing poker with three others, the sheriff watched him curiously and with concern.

Defiantly, Mark poured two more, one immediately after the other. He downed each at a gulp.

Warmth began to course through his stomach. His mind fuzzed. But the intolerable hurt did not leave; it seemed only to increase. This whisky was a bitter, sour taste in his mouth.

He cursed under his breath. Determinedly, he continued to drink. The room began to whirl. His eyes saw everything double. Owlishly, he blinked, fixing his stare on the sheriff.

Healy's face rose through his confused thoughts, and hatred boiled in him. Healy's face faded, to be replaced by the softness of Susan's face. Mark shook his head. This time he didn't bother to pour whisky into his glass. He tipped the bottle and drank until he could drink no more.

He set the bottle back on the table with exaggerated care. The room tipped. He heard a crash, without realizing he had made it himself by falling out of his chair onto the floor. And then he knew no more.

Abruptly, the sheriff left his table and walked to Mark. He stood looking down. Then, bending, he lifted Mark to his feet and steadied him against the wall. Stooping, he put his shoulder hard against Mark's belly and straightened, slinging him across his back.

He went out and walked heavily along the street to the hotel. Panting, he climbed the stairs, entered Mark's room and dumped him on the bed. Looking down, he said sympathetically, "So she wouldn't have you, huh?"

Mark groaned in his sleep. Wearily, the sheriff turned and left the room.

Mark awoke at dawn, sicker than he had ever been in his life before. Immediately, memory of the previous night came rushing back, and with it his intolerable hurt and disappointment. He got up and splashed water into his face. Then he clumped heavily downstairs and paid his bill.

He tramped wearily to the stable. Mounting, he rode out of town, letting his horse have its head. Perhaps, somehow, he could rid himself of hate. At least he could try. And when he had succeeded, he could return—to Susan and to Chimney Rock, if it was not, by then, too late.

Winter howled out of the north, sweeping the southern plains with its icy blasts, piling snow twenty feet deep in the mountains. Spring came, and set the tumbling mountain streams to roaring down their narrow gorges. Summer baked the plains, and fall turned the leaves to gold.

Mark Atkins drifted, aimless and without direction. Month piled upon month, year upon year.

At first he had found, in an empty loneliness that almost frightened him, a reluctance to relinquish hatred, for it provided his life with its motivating force. Later, when he discovered he could think of Healy without the quickened heartbeat, without the flush of automatic anger, he shrank from returning to Chimney Rock, for fear that what he would find might start his hatred burning again.

Susan had probably married. She had sent him away furiously, in anger and humiliation. She had put him firmly out of her life.

Many times did Mark turn his face toward Chimney Rock. As many times as he turn it away. The truth of the matter was that he was afraid—afraid to go back—afraid of what he might find and how he might react.

Healy had probably returned. And if he had, Susan had undoubtedly married him, if only to prove to herself that Mark's accusations had been false and unfounded.

So Mark lived on, going from job to job, saving as carefully as he had saved at Dawson's, only occasionally going on a spree or satisfying his healthy woman-hunger in a brothel.

• • •

When he was twenty-five, he passed within fifty miles of Chimney Rock and on impulse, turned toward it, determined to sever the last of the cords that bound him to the past.

Susan would surely be married now. She was probably fat, with a brood of children crawling about her feet, clinging to the hem of her dress.

Mark examined himself thoughtfully as he rode along. He thought of Healy deliberately, then of Jaime and Rosa María. He discovered that there was nothing left, of hatred for Healy, of grief for the Mexican family who had befriended him. It was gone. It was part of the past.

And yet, not all the past was dead, for Mark found his blood pounding harder as he thought of Susan, as he remembered the soft fire of her lips, the warmth of her strong young body, the gentle tenderness of her eyes.

See her then, he told himself, see her grown placid and plump in the house of another man. See her children. Kill the dream once and for all, and then begin to live again.

The miles were endless, and the hours seemed like days. But at last he rode into Chimney Rock, and it was like the first day he had ridden in more than five years before.

The windmill still turned in the middle of the street. Water overflowed the tank to make a sea of mud around its base. A couple of boys played with a boat on the wind-ruffled surface of the tank.

But there was a change, if not in the town, then in Mark himself. No longer did he wear the gun in a tied-down holster low on his thigh; instead he wore it the way cowmen do, high around his waist.

The look of coldness, of ready deadliness was gone from his eyes, replaced by a friendly, outgoing willingness to take his fellowmen at their face value.

His face was dark, his cowman's clothes worn and gray with dust. He swung down in front of the hotel and tied his horse. He looked across at the sheriff's office, then angled toward it, batting his hat against his leg and raising a cloud of fine red dust.

Though tension was strong in him, he grinned at the sheriff easily. "Remember me?"

The sheriff looked him over, recognition lighting his eyes. "Figured you'da been killed in a gunfight long ago. Looks like you got smart in time. Looks like you've changed."

"And Susan Kerby? How is she, Sheriff? Married?"

The sheriff nodded. "Married and gone. Been gone nearly four years. Got a little girl that ought to be four or five years old. Maybe she's got more'n that for all I know."

"Who'd she marry?" Mark waited for the answer, his hands clenched into tight fists.

"Abe Healy."

Mark turned his back to the sheriff and stared out the dirty window into the dusty street. He had expected this answer, yet its shock was definite, like the blow of a fist in the pit of his stdmach.

The sheriff said, "I bucked you, son, when you were here before. I was wrong. I knew it the night I carried you to the hotel and put you to bed. You wouldn't have hurt her. You'd have been right for her."

Mark said tonelessly, "Where are they now?"

"Town called Arriola, over in southern Colorado, the last I heard. Homesteadin'."

Mark turned. He found he was able to smile. "Thanks, Sheriff."

"Sure. You're welcome. Too bad you stormed out of town when you did. If you'd stayed . . . or if you'da come back sooner . . ."

Mark nodded. He said bitterly, "If!" He went out and stood for a moment in the glaring winter sun. He had found exactly what he had expected to find. Now he could go.

And yet, as he walked toward the hotel, he knew that he couldn't go. He'd started out to run this down and there'd be no peace for him until he had.

With a wry grin, he untied his horse, mounted, and rode away, heading toward the northeast. Five years had passed. He could afford to take another month to kill the dream for good.

Chapter 11

ARRIOLA was a cheerless town in winter. Cotton-woods made their naked tracery against a lead-gray sky. Snow, dirtied by dust and smoke, accumulated in spots sheltered from the sun. The town's business houses along Main all needed paint, all needed their windows washed.

As in Chimney Rock, a windmill stood in the exact center of the main street, in front of Samson's Store, its blades spinning dizzily in the strong, cold wind. From its discharge pipe, a steady stream of water splashed into the tank at the windmill's base.

The only sign of activity on Main came from the two saloons and Samson's Store.

Chilled by his long ride, Mark swung down before the Stockman's Saloon. His eyes swept the street briefly as he looped his reins around the worn and polished rail. Then, scuffing mud from his feet, he went inside.

There was sawdust on the floor. Half a dozen cowmen were at the bar, their sheepskin coats unbuttoned, the scarfs they wore around their ears while riding stuffed carelessly into the pockets of their coats.

Mark stepped up to the bar. "Whisky," he said, and when the bartender had slid glass and bottle to him, he poured himself a drink.

It was warm going down. He shivered and poured another. Then he laid half a dollar on the bar.

The bartender took it and gave him a quarter. Mark said quietly, "I'm looking for a man named Healy. I understand he lives hereabouts. Can you give me directions to his place?"

The bartender shot a glance at the cowmen on Mark's left, almost as though asking permission, but none of them spoke. He turned back to Mark. "Take the east road out of town. The turnoff's five or six miles out—to the left. There's a butte south of the turnoff. You can't miss it."

Mark said, "Thanks." He looked at the bottle for a moment, comfortable for the first time today. Then, shrugging faintly, he turned up his collar and swung toward the door.

The cowmen at the bar were watching him, all of them. He was amused. It appeared that Healy wasn't particularly popular here.

On the windswept plankwalk outside, Mark paused to tie his scarf over his head and under his chin. He crammed his hat down atop it. Untying his reins, he mounted and rode out of town.

In spite of himself, an odd kind of excitement kept rising in him. He was going to see Susan for the first time in more than five years. . . .

At the foot of a high butte on his right he found the turnoff and swung left into it. Nearly grown over with grass, it consisted of no more than a pair of ruts winding out across the plain.

This was homestead country. In the distance, Mark could see several sorry-looking shacks, a patch of plowed ground beside each. He could see fences and an occasional wind-buffeted horse, his rump to the wind, his tail whipping between his legs.

He rode along the twisting tracks for about three miles. He saw it then from a little rise. It had to be Healy's place because the road ended in its yard.

The house was like half a hundred other homestead shacks out on the high plains, hastily constructed, soon to be abandoned. A halfhearted attempt had been made to cultivate a thirty-acre patch on the east side of the house, but apparently that had been abandoned before the plowing was finished. Weeds had grown out of the fifty-foot-wide strip of plowed ground that encircled the patch.

Mark could see the remains of a summer garden immediately in front of the house, but even that was gone now and from the tracks in it, Mark assumed that cattle or horses had eaten it. He could almost imagine Susan pleading with Healy to fence her garden in, could guess at her heartbreak on the morning she had come out to find it trampled to the ground.

Looking at the bleak, cheerless shack, Mark felt sorry for Susan. And angry. He remembered her as she had been five years ago in Chimney Rock, fresh and young, full of life. He imagined the way she must be now. Disheartened, beaten. She had deserved better than this.

He nudged his horse into motion and dismounted beside the barbed-wire horse corral. He tied his reins to the top wire and swung toward the house.

He knocked on the thin panel door, noting that it was warped by the weather for lack of a coat of paint.

He waited, and knocked again. The door opened the merest crack. "What is it?" The voice was Susan's, but he couldn't see her face.

Mark felt anger stir in him. He said, "Susan? It's Mark Atkins." Suddenly he was remembering the way they had parted, and wondered if she still hated him.

"Mark! Is it really you?" She opened the door wide and stood framed in it.

Mark tried to conceal his shock. She looked much older then he remembered her. He could see he had frightened her and fright did not improve her looks. She was pale and shabbily dressed.

"Well, for goodness' sakes, come in, Mark! Abe isn't here, but it's all right," she said, a bit too firmly.

Mark went in and closed the door behind him. The floor was of dirt, hardpacked and worn uneven by much sweeping. It was a rough, unlovely cabin, its only virtue its spotless cleanliness.

A small girl of four or five stared at Mark timorously from a corner and hugged a rag doll. She was a pretty thing, with soft, well-brushed hair, and a dress both too short and too tight for her.

Susan's face flushed with embarrassment. "How did you find us, Mark?"

"I inquired in Chimney Rock, then in Arriola."

"You must be starved. I'll fix you something."

"Thanks. I am hungry," he said gratefully.

The little girl stared at him with something close to fascination. Mark smiled at her encouragingly. Susan said, "This is Abby, Mark. She's not quite four."

Mark realized suddenly that so far neither Susan nor Abby had smiled. He said, "That's a pretty doll, youngster."

Little Abby didn't reply. Her eyes clung to his face. He looked away, confused.

Why had he come? Damn it, why? He'd done himself no good, and he'd embarrassed Susan horribly.

He sat there at the table for what seemed an eternity, and then Susan brought him a plate. The fare was plain, but filling and tasty. Beans, coffee made from scorched beans, bread without butter. Mark ate hungrily, his eyes on his plate.

Susan sat down across from him and Abby peered around her, reminding Mark of a puppy, tail wagging, yearning for affection yet obviously fearing a curse or a blow instead. Hatred for Healy, which he had thought was dead, came rushing back.

Mark suddenly noticed the bruise that darkened Susan's left eye. It was almost healed, which was why he had not noticed it before. To make conversation, he asked, "Did you have a fall, Susan? That's a nasty bruise."

Her instant confusion, the flush that raced over her face, gave Mark his answer. He flushed himself, and dropped his glance to his plate. Abby piped, "Daddy did it, didn't he, Ma?"

Mark looked up, murmuring contritely, "I'm sorry, Susan. I was just trying to make talk." His anger kept rising. Healy was not only a callous killer; he was a petty tyrant, a cowardly bully as well. But Mark could say nothing without giving the impression of "You see? I told you so."

Mark got up, wanting desperately to be gone. He

lounged against the door, the planes of his face hard and flat, his eyes revealing the hard times he'd known.

He smiled at Susan, studying her. "It's good to see you, Susan."

Her eyes gave him her gratitude. And suddenly he was seeing her, not as she was, but as she had been. Her eyes told him that she was not beat, not discouraged, but forever hopeful.

Her lips curved in a gentle smile. "It's been good seeing you, Mark."

She made no reference to their parting. She did not concede that Mark had been right. She did not apologize for her surroundings, nor even for the bruise on her eye.

And Mark discovered something within himself that he'd thought was gone. He realized that nothing was changed except the time and the place. He still loved Susan. He saw in her something that would never die—true beauty that had nothing to do with face or form. It was an irrepressible, gentle courage that stemmed from inner character.

Pale and wan she might be, but her eyes were the eyes of the girl he had known so long ago. He said, "Susan . . ." His throat felt tight as he stepped toward her.

She evaded him. "No, Mark."

He said softly, "I came here so that I could forget you. Now I know I never will."

Her eyes brightened. She blinked and looked away.

"Mark, please go. There is nothing . . ." She stopped when she saw the expression on his face.

He was looking at something hanging on the wall. Wild, ungovernable fury roared through his body. He broke out into a sweat.

Several objects were strung together on the wall, like beads upon a thong—human scalps, dried and shrunk, covered with dust. Mark covered his face with his hands and shuddered.

Susan's voice was barely audible. "I discovered them in his things the day we were married, Mark, and knew you had told the truth. I took them out and buried them, but he made me show him where they were. He dug them up and hung them on the wall."

Mark looked at her incredulously. "And you stayed with him?"

"He's my husband, Mark."

Abby, frightened by the things she saw in their faces, began to whimper softly. Susan asked, "What are you going to do, Mark?"

"It took five years to forget how I hated him," he said. "Now I wonder where the five years went, because I hate him still."

Clenching and unclenching his hands, he fought for self-control. Susan pleaded, "Mark, please go."

"I suppose I should." Almost like a sleepwalker, he went toward the door. Reaching it, he paused and turned.

Susan spoke from across the room. "I'm glad you came, Mark. It's so good to see you, to see the way you've changed. The change is for the better, Mark. Now go away, and don't come back. Forget I ever lived."

There was nothing more to be said. In them both was the full consciousness that Susan was married now and that it was too late. But in them both, as well, was the strong attraction that had always been between them, an attraction which neither could afford to acknowledge.

Susan's determined smile was fading. Her eyes, meeting his, were wide and vulnerable. She said firmly, "Good-by, Mark."

Mark nodded. "Good-by, Susan." He opened the door and stepped into the biting wind. He buttoned his coat and tied the scarf over his head, cramming his hat angrily over it.

She said faintly, her words nearly lost in the rush of the wind, "Good luck."

Nodding, he turned away, stirred by a vague and helpless anger. There was nothing he could do. Nothing. Yet he could not forget the vulnerability that had been in her eyes at the last. He could not still the hunger that was almost like a pain in his body.

He stalked toward the corral furiously, untied his horse and swung into the saddle. Damn Healy! Damn him anyway!

Turning, he glanced toward the house. He caught a flash of white in the window and knew that she had been watching him.

The old excitement stirred, but he did not turn back. Instead he headed out at a gallop along the two-track road toward Arriola.

He knew he would stay there. And he knew he'd see her again.

Perhaps by staying, by being near, he could help her. She needed help—needed it desperately. Living with a man who had killed as callously as Healy had in San Pablo, she might even be in physical danger.

The very thought of Healy hurting her . . .

He began to wonder what he would do if he met Healy now upon the road. He knew he'd want to kill Healy as he'd never wanted anything before. He'd thought his hatred was dead, and perhaps it had been—until he saw Susan. Perhaps now his desire to kill Healy stemmed not from what Healy had done in San Pablo, but from what he had done to Susan.

And suppose he did kill Healy? What then? Would Susan's principles, her conscience, allow her to marry the man who had killed her husband? Mark didn't think so. And even if she could bring herself to it, there would be guilt in her because of it, perhaps enough to ruin forever their chance of happiness.

I should never have come here, thought Mark. I should never have come. Scowling, he rode along, unconscious of the driving wind, unconscious of the stinging flakes of snow. . .

He put up his horse at the livery barn in Arriola and tramped through the inch-deep snow to the saloon. He went in and bought himself a drink. Then, taking the bottle, he walked to a table in the corner and sat down, alone.

The cowmen who had been at the bar were still there. Occasionally one of them glanced toward him curiously.

Mark paid no attention, his mind busy with the problem confronting him.

He had finished a fourth of the bottle when he saw one of the cowmen turn from the bar and come toward him.

The man was thin, his hair graying. His eyes, deep-set in their sockets, were calm and friendly. There was a light stubble of graying whiskers on the man's face, and he wore a small, clipped mustache. He stopped at Mark's table and said, "I'm Phil Straight. Did you find the Healy place?"

Mark nodded.

"Healy home?"

Mark looked at Straight curiously. He shook his head.

Straight stood uncertainly there for a moment, then turned to go. He changed his mind and swung back. "Staying in the country, or passing through? Not that it's any of my business."

Mark liked the man. He said, "I don't know." He stood up and stuck out his hand. "I'm Mark Atkins. Will you sit down?"

Straight sat down, grinning, a bit uneasy. "Excuse all the questions, but are you a friend of Healy's?"

"No!" It was too emphatic, and Straight's smile lost

140

its uneasiness. He got up. "If you stay, you'll understand why I was so damn nosy. Sorry." He turned and went back to the bar where he resumed his conversation with his friends.

Mark poured himself another drink.

Chapter 12

MARK awoke the next morning in a room at the hotel. His head was splitting and he had a bitter, cottony taste in his mouth. He didn't remember coming here.

He sat up cautiously, holding his throbbing head in his hands. He stood, then, and walked to the window.

A foot of new snow lay on the ground outside, marred only by a few early wagon and buggy tracks. A team, standing before the Stockman's Saloon, blew clouds of frosty breath into the still, cold air.

Mark's thoughts focused instantly. How, he wondered, was Susan faring this morning? Had Healy returned? And if he had not, did Susan have enough wood to keep the stove warm? Was there enough food in the house?

His face twisted violently. He'd drive himself crazy if he continued like this. What he needed to do, and soon, was to find himself something that would keep him busy—a job, a ranch, anything that would keep his mind occupied and away from that nagging, insoluble problem.

He washed in the icy water from the pitcher on the

141

washstand. He shaved with it angrily, enjoying the vicious pull of his razor. Then he dressed and went downstairs.

He breakfasted in the hotel dining room, remembering another dining room and another waitress. Afterward he wandered around town through the deep, soft snow until he saw an office whose sign read, *Attorney—Real Estate.*

He went in. "I want to buy a small ranch. Have you got anything?"

The man behind the desk was elderly, a gaunt, big-boned man whose skin was like old saddle leather. He got up and squeezed Mark's hand briefly. "The name's Bill Robinson. Got several. How much do you want to pay?"

"I've got twelve hundred." Mark had the currency strapped in a belt around his waist, all his savings.

"Might have just the place. One I'm thinkin' of is over on Blue Creek. Not much in the way of buildings, but there's lots of good grass—an' water. Fifty-sixty head of stock are supposed to go with it."

Mark said, "How much?"

"Well, let's see." Robinson riffled the scattered papers on his desk. "Used to belong to Frank DuBois. He was killed six months ago and his widow went East. Cattle may be scattered, but likely they're all there. Eighteen dollars a head—an' you pay only for what you tally."

"Fair enough."

Robinson continued to search. He came up at last

with a scrap of an envelope. Figures were written haphazardly all over it. He said, "Nine hundred is the price of the place. Four homestead claims deeded— that's six hundred and forty. Four thousand acres of grass claimed and held. Say fifty head of cattle at eighteen dollars, not countin' calves. Looks like the whole shebang would come to about eighteen hundred. You could borrow half of that easy enough at the bank. Leave you three hundred to operate on."

Mark said, "Sounds all right. Let's go look."

Robinson put on his hat, a battered Stetson, and got a heavy bearskin coat from the coat tree. Mark went out with him and Robinson locked the door.

They walked through the deep snow toward the livery barn. A few of the town's storekeepers were shoveling their walks. All looked up and spoke pleasantly to Robinson. They stared at Mark curiously.

They're wondering why I'm here, he thought. Sooner or later, they would know. They'd know that Mark wanted Abe Healy's wife.

And what if Abe found out? Mark's jaws clenched. Healy must never find out. Because if he did, he'd make Susan's life intolerable.

When they arrived at the stable, Robinson hired horses for them both. They mounted and rode out.

Riding in silence, Robinson took the east road, the one that led to Healy's homestead shack. But he turned off to the left long before they reached the foot of the butte.

This road was probably little better than Healy's

143

two-track lane. In fact Mark could see evidences of a road only where it angled across the face of a low hill, or bridged a dry arroyo.

They climbed steadily until midmorning, passing through a mass of low hills and dropping at last in a long, wide valley through which a stream ran, black against the glaring whiteness of the snow. Mark saw the dark shapes of cattle scattered on the hills, and occasionally the gray, fleeting shape of a coyote.

"Nice country, ain't it Mr. . . . . Hell, I didn't get your name."

"It's Mark Atkins. And it is a nice country. Although a man's a damn fool to buy a ranch with a foot of snow on it."

"Wait till the snow melts off, if you want. I'd rather see you satisfied than anything else."

Mark didn't reply. In the distance he could see the buildings, nestled in the lee of a bluff, protected from the bitter winter winds. A spring welled out of the ground behind the house and ran past it, channeled into a corral tank by means of a V-shaped trough.

The house was not much better than Healy's shack. The barn sat askew, having settled heavily on the downhill side.

Mark looked at it approvingly. Better that the buildings were poor; rebuilding them would give him hard, physical work to do. It would take him time. It would dull his mind with fatigue, and make him sleep like the dead at night.

They rode into the yard and dismounted. Mark

144

noted that there was a solid rock foundation under the house, and a wide, solidly built stone fireplace.

He looked around. "Where does the land lie?"

Robinson grinned. "I'll show you the best I can." He pointed. "North there, it corners on that high bluff, about a mile behind the house. Runs east from there about four miles to Blue Creek. Then south two miles. Can't see no marker on that from here. Then west roughly to the point of the bluff about two miles southwest of here. Then back to the point of beginning. Close to eight square miles in all. Plenty for a man to run up to about five-six hundred head of cattle."

Mark said, "Let's go see the banker. If he'll go nine hundred, I'll take it."

Riding back, he could not get the ranch on Blue Creek out of his thoughts. His mind kept seeing the house he would build, a stout, strong house of spruce logs. His mind kept seeing a door open, kept seeing Susan come from it to stand on the stoop and wave.

Reaching town in early afternoon, Robinson rode directly to the bank, a small, stone building on the corner across from the hotel.

And there Mark closed the deal, signing a note for nine hundred, paying another nine hundred out of the currency in his moneybelt. He left the deed with the banker for safekeeping.

After that, he went to the livery barn and hired a buckboard. He drove it to Samson's Store, went in and bought enough supplies to last a month. He bought nails and a hammer, a saw, a double-bitted ax and a trowel.

Samson, a stocky, short man with a full beard, helped him carry the stuff out to the buckboard. Then Mark drove out of town.

It was dark when he arrived. He unloaded the buckboard, unhitched and watered the team. He put them in the draughty barn and threw down hay for them from the loft. He judged there was about a ton of hay in the loft—scarcely enough to winter his saddle horse.

It wouldn't be easy, but he didn't want it easy. He wanted it hard—hard enough to make him stop dreaming of Susan—hard enough to make him stop needing and wanting her.

The house was cold and musty. Mark spread his blankets on the creaking bedsprings and slept until dawn.

He made himself some breakfast, then wandered from room to room, inspecting the house. It would have to be torn down. So would the barn. Between the two, he could work like a madman until spring.

He went out and hitched up the buckboard. Then he drove toward town. It began to snow again.

He returned the team and got his saddle horse. He tied it in front of the hotel while he had his dinner. Then he mounted and started back toward the edge of town.

When he saw Abe Healy driving his wagon into town, he reined over to the rail in front of the

Stockman's Saloon. He swung down and fished under his coat for the makings. It was not only the cold that made his fingers like thumbs as he tried to separate a single paper from the pack. He managed it, but his fingers trembled noticeably as he shook flake tobacco into the tiny trough of paper.

He licked the cigarette, sealed it and stuck it between his lips. He raked a match along the rough surface of his sheepskin. Cupping his hands around it, he touched the flame to the cigarette tip and raised his eyes.

Healy wore a beard, which hid the lower part of his face. He was heavier than he had been the last time Mark had seen him in San Pablo. But his eyes were the same. He was the same Abe Healy, and the intervening ten years had stamped his face with deep lines of cruelty.

Looking at him, Mark felt as though his heart had stopped, as though the blood had stilled and begun to cool in his veins. He knew that if he did not take his eyes from Healy's face, he would do something violent.

Pulling his eyes away was one of the hardest things he had ever done. Deliberately, he looked at Susan.

She sat beside her husband, her fine shoulders defiantly straight. Her eyes were fixed steadily on a rosette in the breeching straps. The blue bruise on her cheekbone was very noticeable this afternoon. Her color was high, but Mark could not have said whether that was caused by the long ride in the cold wind or because she had seen him. Little Abby, subdued and silent, sat wrapped in blankets in the back of the wagon cuddling the rag doll.

Mark straightened as the wagon drew abreast, and with a wide-armed swing, threw the match into the street. The gesture summed up his frustration and his anger.

The wagon went past him. Mark did not have to look at her any more. He had memorized each small feature of her face, from the full but pale lips, to the eyes, so resigned now, so filled with quiet acceptance. He closed his eyes and still could see the sweet curve of her cheek, the proud column of her throat, the soft, dark hair brushed back into a demure bun on her neck. But she was like a train on a steel track. There were no turnoffs now, and few stops, only continuation to a predetermined end.

Mark himself was on another track, paralleling hers but never joining it. There was murder in his glance as it rested on the broad, muscled back of Abe Healy. He was trembling visibly with the effort he made at holding himself in. It was as though the town did not exist, nor the people in it. It was as if the world consisted of these four, Susan, Abby, Abe Healy and himself, and the inevitably certain trouble that must be the end of this for them.

Phil Straight's voice spoke quietly at Mark's elbow.

"It's a damned shame, the way he treats that wife of his. . . . You ain't been here long, Mr. Atkins, but you'd just as well know what Healy is. He's a rustler."

Mark swung around, anger plain in his slate-gray eyes. "If you know that, why the hell don't you do something about it?" He studied Straight, wondering how much the man had guessed. Straight must have seen the hatred in Mark's eyes.

But Straight's glance was steady, saying no more than his words had said. He replied, "We've never been able to get any proof. But the time will come when we will. And then we'll string him up."

Mark scowled. It was as though Straight had said, "We'll hang Healy, and you can have his woman." Or perhaps Straight wasn't thinking that at all. Perhaps it was only the guilt in Mark's soul that made him assume Straight was. The surging hope that had been born in him at Straight's words only served to increase his guilt.

Mark said deliberately, "I'm new here. It's not my problem."

"That's where you're wrong. It's every cowman's problem. It has to be."

Mark tossed his cigarette onto the snowy boardwalk. It hissed as it died in the snow. Phil Straight stared at Mark's scowling face for a moment. Then he slapped Mark's shoulder companionably and turned away to re-enter the saloon.

Upstreet, Abe Healy drew his team to a halt before Samson's Store. Susan climbed down, then raised her arms to Abby, standing in the back. Susan's coat was shabby and thin. She looked miserably cold. She stood for a moment talking to Abe and then climbed the steps to the walk before Samson's Store.

Her hesitation at the door told Mark as plainly as words could have done that Abe had given her no money, that she hated going inside with no slight excuse to justify her presence there. Mark would have made a bet that she didn't have enough to buy Abby even a sack of candy.

Abe drove the wagon to the far end of the street, and without unhitching, tied the team to a cottonwood. He turned away from the wagon and walked back. He went into the door at Solomon's, the farmer's saloon.

Mark jerked himself erect and took a step toward Samson's Store. He halted himself at once. It wouldn't do. It just wouldn't do. By seeing her, he would only make things harder for her.

He swung around and went into the Stockman's Saloon. He got a bottle and glass at the bar and carried them to a table against the wall. He raised the brimming glass to his lips, but today just the smell of liquor brought waves of nausea to his stomach. He set it down untouched.

Phil Straight came toward him, and Mark looked up. Phil said, "You'll be needing help to get settled out on the Blue. I'll bring my hired man and come over tomorrow."

Straight was friendly and sincere. Mark grinned at him. "That's good of you. The place is in a hell of a shape. I could use some help."

"I'll see Mel Woolery sometime today. Maybe he

could come help too. What're you going to do, try and repair the house?"

Mark shook his head. "I'm going to tear it down and rebuild with logs. How far does a man have to go to get spruce logs?"

"There's a patch of them on the bluff in back of your house. I'll bring a team tomorrow and we'll start getting them off."

Mark had a drink with Straight, which he didn't want, then returned the bottle to the bar. Going out, he mounted and, without even glancing up the street, rode out toward home.

However much misery and frustration lay ahead, he was glad now that he was staying. Perhaps Susan would never belong to him, but he would be here in case she needed help.

Chapter 13

ON THE FOLLOWING MORNING, at sunup, Mark saw Straight and two other men coming up the road. Straight led a harnessed team. Grinning cheerfully, he dismounted and tied his saddle horse. Then he tied the team. The other two also dismounted and came forward to meet Mark. Straight introduced them.

Mel Woolery was an enormous man, six feet six inches tall. His face was round and cheerful and massive. He grinned at Mark and boomed, "Atkins? Glad to know you. My MW outfit lies about ten miles southeast, the other side of that flat where the homesteaders are. Now let's get goin'. Whadda you want to do first?"

Mark said, smiling back and liking this giant, "First we'll drink a cup of coffee. Come on in. It's a boar's nest, though."

He shook hands with the other man, Straight's hired hand. Todd McFee was a wizened, bowlegged man who looked as though he'd been born in a saddle.

Mark led the way into the kitchen. He poured coffee into rusty tin cups, and they drank it gustily. After that, they went outside, gathered tools and set out for the top of the bluff.

All day, Mark swung an ax, pushing himself to get trees down and trimmed fast enough to keep the others busy skidding them to the bottom. Woolery and McFee each drove a single skid horse, walking to the bottom and riding the horse back to the top. Straight worked a hundred yards away, also felling trees.

At noon, when they rode in for dinner, there were nearly forty logs lying in the snow beside Mark's corral. And when they quit at sundown there were close to a hundred.

He tried to talk them out of coming again tomorrow, but they wouldn't hear of it, assuring him they would be around until he had enough logs skidded in to build his house.

Mark went to bed so tired he slept almost the instant his head touched the pillow.

The next day followed the pattern of the last. And the days blended into a routine of work and meals and sleep, while the pile of logs grew steadily.

At last, on the night of the fifth day, Woolery and Straight told him they'd not be back again. At least not until he needed help to raise the logs.

He thanked them, feeling a comradeship with them he'd not felt with anyone since the death of Chester Ewing. He said earnestly, "When you need some help yourselves, you let me know. I owe you more . . ."

Woolery boomed, "Forget it, man. What're neighbors for, except to help? Besides, we wasn't doin' nothin' at home but sittin' around the stove." They rode off, taking their team.

Mark began to cut and notch the logs to size, laying them carefully on all sides of the house until he had enough to build each wall.

The days passed in lonely monotony, one after the other. The snow melted off, and more fell, and that melted off as well. Warm winds blew out of the south, alternating with an occasional cold one from the north. Susan Healy's face never quite disappeared from Mark's thoughts, but so tired did he keep himself, and so busy, that he had little time to let them dwell upon her.

With the logs ready, he stored the furniture and household effects in the barn, and began to tear down the house. He carefully saved whatever lumber was usable, and pulled and straightened all the nails.

Occasionally Woolery or Straight stopped by to

drink coffee with him and pass on bits of local gossip. Rustlers were still busy, they said, but so cleverly did they operate that no one had been able to catch them with the goods. Usually they carried out their raids during a snowstorm, so that their tracks would be covered and impossible to follow.

Straight's young wife had had a baby. Todd McFee had fallen from a horse and wrenched his back. Mark listened smilingly, his feeling of closeness to these two men increasing with the passing weeks.

When he got the house torn down, they helped him raise the walls, helped him place the rafters. Then they went away again.

But the work went on. Patiently, endlessly, Mark worked. Never a carpenter, he learned to be one, and a good one. He did his work meticulously, for somewhere in the back of his mind was the thought that this house had to be perfect. It had to be solid and warm and safe. It had to be comfortable.

Spring came, and Mark rode with the other cattlemen on roundup. He branded, glorying in the back-breaking, dusty, sweaty work. He welcomed the ache that crept into his bones and stayed. He welcomed the hard jerk of a full-grown steer hitting the end of his rope. He punished himself deliberately, staying in the saddle twelve or fourteen hours a day so that when he hit his bedroll, he dropped off to sleep immediately from numbed exhaustion.

Yet even with this self-punishment, he still had time to think of Susan. He was strong and virile, and sometimes the hunger grew in him until it was nearly intolerable.

He lost weight. He grew irritable and short-tempered, though mostly with himself and seldom toward Straight or Woolery.

Summer came, and he rode a mower in his hay meadow, or a rake, or stood upon the stack as the stacker dumped load after load down upon it.

He fought continually with his desire to see her again, if only to look at her, to see if she was content or as miserable as he was himself. Sometimes, against his better judgment, he inquired after her from Straight or Woolery, but their answer was always the same: "She looks all right, Mark." And then they'd look away, as if afraid their eyes would reveal what they thought of a man who would covet another man's wife. Or maybe that was only Mark's guilt at work again.

When late summer eliminated the need for further farm and cattle work, Mark cut more logs on the bluff and skidded them in to rebuild the barn. He dug a root cellar and walled it with stone hauled in a wagon from a sandstone quarry five miles back into the hills. He fenced his meadow, and repaired his corral.

At last, in desperation, he went to Arriola, to the Stockman's Saloon. He got drunk and stayed that way for a week.

He saw her face in the strangest places, on the round, white face of the moon at night, in the clear, rippling water of the creek at the edge of town, in the dark lobby of the hotel in early morning.

But he didn't like himself when he reeked of whisky and stale sweat. And he found no solution to his problem in the bottles behind the bar of the Stockman's Saloon. Disgusted with himself, he left the place and returned to the hotel.

He slept, and spent the whole next day sobering up. His hands were shaky as he shaved, and he cut himself three times. He went to Samson's Store and bought himself a new pair of jeans and a flannel shirt. With these on, he got his horse at the livery barn, saddled and rode along the road toward home.

It was early fall. Grass on the prairie was dry and long. It waved in the wind like wheat, a fascinating, rippling, ever-changing movement.

Mark cursed himself bitterly and called himself a fool. He should never have stayed in this country. There was nothing here for him except frustration and misery. He'd been here nearly a year, and Susan had not needed him. Perhaps she would never need him. He should have left that first day, and put her out of his mind.

Thinking of her, he rode around a bend in the road.

She and little Abby were alone at the side of the road, their wagon canted at an angle, one of its rear wheels broken off at the axle. Mark rode up, his face unsmiling and expressionless to conceal the excitement and yearning that churned in his heart. "Hello, Susan. Trouble?"

She had been crying. Now she looked up and

hastily dabbed at her eyes with a tiny handkerchief. Her face was smudged with grease from the axle. Her hands were dirty and her dress was torn.

Apparently she had tried to lift the wagon by herself. She said helplessly, "I tried to fix it, but I'm not strong enough. I guess I couldn't have fixed it anyway. It's broken off."

Mark dismounted. He knelt to look at the broken axle. A faint aura of woman fragrance drifted into his nostrils. He glanced up at once. She was kneeling too, looking at the broken axle and the furrow it had plowed in the hard-packed road. Abby had wandered off and was chasing one of the tiny, incredibly fast lizards that abounded in the country.

Susan looked up, feeling Mark's glance upon her. Their eyes locked desperately.

Mark stood up. He reached down and helped her to her feet.

It was the first time he had touched her since he had left her in Chimney Rock six years ago. Even through the thickness of dress and coat, the touch was electric. For a timeless instant he stared into her eyes, his hands tightening involunatrily on her arms.

Nothing existed in the world, for now, but this man and woman. He could recall no movement, no movement at all. But suddenly she was in his arms, held hard against his powerful chest. His lips were against hers, hungry and demanding.

She cried, "No! Oh no!" and fought to break away. He let her go, though fire soared in his brain.

Mark said hoarsely, "I'm sorry, Susan." He looked at her for a moment, and then he said, "No, I'm not either. Do you know how often I've thought of you in the past few months? Do you know how much I've wanted to ride over and see you?"

Her voice was almost inaudible. "I know, Mark. I know how much I've wanted you to. But you mustn't do it, not ever."

He opened his mouth to argue, but stopped when she raised her face to his. There were tears in her eyes and she was obviously trying to control herself. "Mark, would you ride back to town and have an axle sent out?" She hesitated briefly, flushing slowly and painfully. "No, don't do that. I have no money and I'm sure Abe has no credit left."

Without looking again at Mark, she hurried to the side of the road. She caught Abby by the hand, leading the child back up the road toward Healy's homestead shack.

Never had Mark hated Healy more than at this instant. Abby wailed, "Mamma, do we got to walk?"

Mark swung to his saddle and trotted after them. When he reached Susan, he swung down and, leading the horse, fell into step beside her. He said, "Susan, you're acting like a child. I'd offer the same help to any woman I found stranded on the road. Let me help you."

"After what just happened?" Her words were a reproof, but there was no reproof in her glance.

He said harshly, "You can't walk all the way home.

It's several miles. You'd be carrying the little girl before you'd gone a mile."

"It's the only way."

He seized her arm and pulled her to a halt. He grinned. "You were always stubborn."

Her face flushed. "Mark, please. Don't taunt me with the past."

"Taunt you? Oh, my God!"

She pulled away and began to walk again. Mark caught her and stopped her a second time. Little Abby looked at them in bewilderment.

Mark felt his anger rise. "Damn it," he said, "any man would do what I want to do for you. Don't be a fool! Do you think I'm the kind who would expect to be repaid for helping you?"

There was a certain ridiculousness about this situation that did not escape him. Apparently it now struck Susan for the first time. She smiled. "I am being silly. And I can't walk home. All right, Mark. We'll wait at the wagon. But whatever is needed, charge it to Abe. Tell them I'll see that the bill is paid."

He mounted his horse. He could see that she did not expect anyone in Arriola to fix Abe Healy's wagon on credit. But he could also see that her pride was very important to her. He turned and rode away reluctantly, wanting to stay, but knowing if he did they would both be sorry.

Riding, he puzzled at himself. What was it about Susan that had so enslaved him? Was it a blind kind of love that knew no reason? Or was it instinct, telling him that here was a woman with more to give than any he had seen before, or would ever see again?

Scowling, he shook his head. He kicked his horse into a gallop, furious both at himself and at Susan. He doubted if ever a man had possessed more justification for killing another. He doubted if ever a man had lived who needed killing more than Abe Healy. And yet, Mark was helpless, for he could never go to Susan with her husband's blood on his hands, nor could he ask for Abby's love if he had killed her father. No matter what Healy was, what he had done or would do, he had to be allowed to live.

At the edge of town, Mark slowed his horse. He rode to the livery stable first. Nat Lowry looked up at him questioningly. "Thought you were headed home. You ought to lay off . . ." He stopped, embarrassed.

Mark grinned. "I'm not staying, Nat. I'm off the bust I was on. It's Abe Healy's wife. She's stranded out on the road. Send a buggy out to her so she can get home, will you?"

"What about . . ."

Mark said, "I'll pay it if Healy won't." He tossed Lowry a half-dollar. "Here's something to pay a kid for driving it out. Tell him to wait at the wagon and he can ride back in with Hugh Neff, after Hugh gets the wagon fixed."

He thought Lowry looked at him curiously, but recognized the possibility that he was imagining it. He turned and rode to Hugh Neff's blacksmith shop.

Neff, a broad-shouldered, black-browed man, was

160

shoeing a horse. Mark rode up and asked, "Can you take an axle out to fix Healy's wagon, Hugh? It's a couple of miles from town."

"And wait forever to get paid? Uh-uh."

Mark said, "I'll pay you if Healy won't."

Neff looked up, questioningly. Mark felt his anger stir. He said, perhaps more emphatically than was necessary, "I don't like Abe Healy a damn bit better than you do. But I used to know his wife. Now let it go at that, will you?"

Neff shrugged and turned away. Mark headed out of town again, this time cutting across country toward home.

Home! The word was a joke. His ranch wouldn't ever be home. It was only a place to sleep and work and dream. It would never be anything else.

Chapter 14

ROUNDUP began in October, and for two weeks Mark rode with the others, ranging as far south as the Twin Buttes, north to Alkali Flats, and west as far as the mining camp at Crooked River.

When he returned, driving his small herd before him, he looked down wearily from the bluff top at the results of his past year's labors.

The house nestled snugly against the foot of the bluff. The spring now ran into a tank above the house, from which it was piped inside. The barn, though not yet chinked, held a dozen tons of hay.

Haystacks, like fat, brown loaves, dotted the meadow. Around each was a tight, barbed-wire fence to keep the cattle out.

Looking down, he realized that in spite of his frustration in regard to Susan, he had found more peace, more solid satisfaction here than he had ever known anywhere else. He had found friends, good, solid, lasting friends. He had forgotten what it was like to live in danger of Apache raids, of other men. He had forgotten, or almost forgotten, how to hate.

He had something to offer Susan now—something more than a nomadic, shiftless existence, something more than vengeance.

He would see her. He would make her discard her old-fashioned notions about the sanctity of marriage. What was sacred about a union with a man who was brutal and selfish, who beat his wife and who withered the soul of his small daughter?

He'd make her see reason! He'd make her see that Healy had not changed—that he was still the man who had slaughtered a dozen people for the value of their scalps—that he was still dishonest, and would inevitably decorate a gallows leaving his wife and daughter penniless behind.

And supposing Healy was at home? Would Mark be able to control the hatred that boiled in his heart every time he glimpsed the man? He knew suddenly that if Healy was at home, he'd simply leave and return another day. He couldn't risk facing Abe Healy, or talking to him. He thought he'd mastered his hatred, but he'd never be sure. Besides, if Healy so much as suspected that Mark was interested in Susan, that he had known her before in Chimney Rock, he'd make her life a living hell.

Mark pushed his cattle off the bluff and shoved them into the fenced meadow. Dismounting, he put up the gate. He rode to the house and washed and shaved and changed his clothes. Then he remounted and set out down the valley.

He moved along steadily and in late afternoon reached the rise behind the Healy shack.

He dismounted and tied his horse to a clump of brush behind the rise. Then, moving cautiously, he topped the bluff and lay down in the warm grass to wait.

For half an hour he lay in the autumn sunlight, and stared down. In the yard outside the shack, clothes fluttered on a makeshift clothesline. A light plume of smoke climbed from the tin chimney. Abby played in the soft dust before the door. The corral held a single horse.

Finally Susan came out carrying a basket, and began to take down the clothes. Otherwise, not even a chicken stirred. A hawk wheeled overhead, gave the yard a brief inspection, then soared away.

Satisfied at last that Healy was not home, Mark returned to his horse and mounted. He rode over the knoll and down the slope.

Susan looked up while he was yet two hundred yards away. For the barest instant, there was gladness and pleasure and welcome in her face. It faded quickly, to be replaced by alarm that was almost panic.

As he rode close, she said, "Please, Mark. Please go away. I don't want to see you. I don't want to talk to you. I'm Abe's wife, and I'll not . . ."

Mark's voice was harsh. "Nobody's asking you to do anything wrong." He lowered his voice so that Abby would not hear. "I'll give you some money. Go away from here. Go to Denver, or Santa Fe or Cheyenne. Get a divorce from him. Then write me and I'll come for you."

He could see it was no good. All the sordid tales of desertion she had ever heard were plainly running through her mind. He said urgently, "My God, Susan, don't you understand? I love you. It doesn't need to be a thing you're ashamed of. There is nothing in your marriage contract that says he can beat you with his fists, that says he can leave you and Abby alone and hungry while he drinks himself unconscious in town."

He stayed on his horse, though every instinct in him told him to get down, to take her in his arms. Yet this would have been unfair, as well he knew. If love was as strong in her as it was in him, her resolve would melt and she might hate him later because he had made her betray her beliefs. Her decision, whatever it was, must come from a clear head or it would be no good.

He said, "I've thought of nothing but you for

164

months. I've tried forgetting in work and I've tried to drown the thought of you in liquor. But it doesn't work. It can't go on. I'll meet him on the street one day—and I'll kill him."

Her eyes widened as she looked at him. She seemed to be trying to search his soul. She asked, "Why, Mark? Because he killed the Ortegas in San Pablo, or because he married me?"

Mark's face twisted. "I don't know." And he didn't. He couldn't separate Healy who had married Susan from Healy who had killed Jaime Ortega and Rosa María. They were one and the same man.

No more could he separate his own hatreds. He had thought he had stopped hating Healy for the killings in San Pablo. Now he was not so sure. Perhaps his hatred had never died. Perhaps . . .

He said steadily, "Will you do it, Susan?"

She shook her head. "No." She tried to smile. "I think you knew what my answer would be, didn't you, Mark? And I think you knew why."

A streak of stubbornness made Mark ask, "Why?"

Susan murmured, looking at the ground, "Marriage is not a thing to be discarded because things do not go right. Abe is the man I married. Perhaps he needs me more now than he did when I married him. Should I desert him because something better comes along for me?"

Mark's shoulders drooped. He had expected no more than this. He had only hoped. He said softly, "I had to ask, Susan."

"I know, Mark. And I'm glad you did. It will be something for me to remember." Her eyes sparkled suddenly with tears. Mark made a move to dismount, but she backed away. "No, Mark."

He looked down at her for a moment more. Abby came from her playing and smiled up at him shyly. Mark said, "Good-by, Abby," but the little girl did not answer. She buried her face in her mother's skirt.

Mark whirled his horse and rode away. He looked back as he left the yard. Susan stood very straight, her dress molded against her body by the wind. She raised an arm and waved, but Mark did not wave back, for he was fixing in his mind this picture of her, this picture, which was all he would ever have.

In early November, Mark arose one morning to a bitter wind howling out of the north, to a leaden sky, to cattle bawling around the fenced stockyards. Going to the door, he saw a rider coming up the road.

He built up the fire and got the coffee started. Then he went outside to wash. By the time he had finished, the rider, Phil Straight, came into the yard and halted, peering around him approvingly. "Man, you've sure changed this place."

Mark nodded, thinking how useless it had been, how pointless. He said, "Get down and come in. The coffee's hot."

Straight dismounted gratefully. Rubbing his chilled hands together, he followed Mark inside, and again he looked around approvingly.

Mark poured coffee and started the breakfast of steaks and potatoes liberally sprinkled with rendered beef tallow.

Sipping his coffee, he studied Straight, whose face was unusually solemn. He asked, "What's eating you?"

Straight hesitated. Then he said, "Roundup tally showed my gather damn near a hundred and fifteen steers short, and that's too many. It's going to make living mighty slim next year."

Mark asked, "You missing all those since spring?"

Straight shook his head. "That's a year's loss. We don't get much of a tally in the spring, because we never really gather."

"Where do you figure they are?"

Straight's face turned grim. "I know where they went. And I know when. We don't lose but a few head in the summer. We lose 'em in the winter, to rustlers. And by God, we're not going to lose any more."

Mark was silent. He was five head short himself, but he had attached no particular significance to it. It didn't hurt him. He had more than he needed anyway. But Straight's circumstances were different. Straight had a family.

Straight asked, "How many are you out?"

"Five is all. How about the others?"

"It's the same all over. Joe Weems is out about twenty—all steers. Joe's got seven kids and a big mortgage at the bank. Joe is hurt. Woolery is out over two hundred, most of them steers. I guess he's the only one who can really afford the loss, but he's sure as hell not happy about it. But you notice one thing. Most of what we're missing is steers, and what ain't steers could be normal summer loss. You see what it adds up to, don't you?"

Mark nodded. "About four hundred head—all steers. It adds up to some pretty damned busy rustlers. Where do the cattle go?"

"The mining camp over at Crooked River. At least that's what we think."

"Can't you stop it there?"

Straight shook his head. "We've tried. But the storekeeper over there is in with 'em. Besides, he don't buy any beef on the hoof. He buys meat. The rustlers stop in some canyon on their way and butcher the stolen cattle on the spot. Then they load the meat in a wagon and haul it in to Crooked River." He shook his head. "No. The only way to catch 'em is right here, before they get the drive into the mountains."

Mark waited. Straight sipped his coffee thoughtfully for a few moments. Then he said, "And Abe Healy spends gold eagles in Solomon's Saloon."

Mark suddenly felt trapped. He was going to be asked to help, and could refuse neither Straight nor Woolery. He owed them too much. They had come to him a year ago and given generously of themselves to help him get started. He'd ridden with them on roundup, and he'd traded work with them during haying. They were his friends.

Straight went on, "Healy hasn't made a crop since he came here five years ago. He hasn't worked, either."

Mark's thoughts withdrew, but Straight pulled them back. "You're in this, Mark. You're one of us. If we hope to stop this goddam rustlin', we've got to stand together. There's an army of thievin' homesteaders down on the flats. If we don't do something about them this winter, they'll clean us out—and you, too."

Mark met his glance. Straight's eyes were hard and uncompromising. Mark nodded wearily. "All right. What are you going to do?"

"We're having a meeting tonight in the Stockman's Saloon. Eight o'clock. We want you to be there."

"All right, Phil. I'll be there."

He gave Straight some breakfast, and even though Straight protested that he'd eaten earlier at home, he put it all away. Afterward he got up and put on his sheepskin coat. "I've got to see some of the others, Mark. Time to stop this is now, before they get a single steer. It's lookin' like snow today, and if it does snow, they'll probably make a raid. We want to catch them when they do."

He went out, mounted and rode down the valley. Mark drank another cup of coffee and washed the dishes. Then he put on his coat and wandered outside. In the barn he curried and fed his horses. With a manure fork, he cleaned out the barn.

Looking out into the meadow, he saw that the cattle had breeched one of the stockyard fences, so he saddled and rode out to fix the fence.

It took him until noon. All the time his mind was like a squirrel in a squirrelcage, running around and around, getting nowhere. He went into the house and moodily prepared a dinner he didn't want.

In midafternoon, it began to snow, fine, sifting flakes driven along on a gale-sized wind. The cattle turned their backs to it and dropped their heads patiently to wait it out. Some of them began to drift out of the meadow, seeking the canyons and bluffs for shelter.

Mark stood at his window, staring out, thinking of Healy, and of Susan. He thought of Straight and Woolery and Weems, all his friends. He felt caught in a trap.

At dusk, he mounted and rode toward town, traveling with deliberate slowness, as though he could delay what he knew was coming. How could he join with the others to catch and hang Healy? How could he, who wanted Healy dead more than any of the others, permit himself to contribute to Healy's death?

And yet, neither could he refuse Straight and Woolery their first request for help.

He grinned sourly to himself. Damned if life didn't have a way of putting a man into impossible situations.

He rode into town and put his horse up at the livery stable. Then he walked up the street toward the Stockman's Saloon.

The wind seemed to have increased its intensity. It howled among the buildings in town, somewhere banging a loose shutter with monotonous regularity.

Snow sifted like desert sand along the boardwalk. There was only about half an inch on the ground now, but the flakes were becoming larger, and falling more thickly than they had before.

Lamplight flickered weakly from the windows of the stores on Main. Here and there a man or woman traveled, head down, collar turned up against the buffeting wind.

In the Stockman's Saloon, the potbellied stove had been fired up and now stood in the center of the room, glowing red-hot.

Mark went to it and held out his numbed hands to its welcome warmth. He glanced around the room.

The meeting hadn't started, but all the cowmen were here, Straight, Woolery, Weems, Woolery's hired man, Slim Hankins and Todd McFee, Straight's hired man. There were some others, too, whom Mark had met on roundup, men from the foothills at the edge of the mountains, from the arid country up near the alkali flats.

Mark went to the bar and ordered a drink. He downed it and Straight, at his elbow, said, "We're all here. Let's head for the back room."

Straight moved about the room, speaking to one after another of the cowmen. Mark left the bar, but a touch on his elbow made him stop. He looked around and saw Hugh Neff, the blacksmith, standing there uncertainly. He said, "Hello, Hugh. What's on your mind?"

Straight had returned, and now stood a few feet away, waiting for Mark.

Neff said, "I guess I should forget it, Mark, but Nellie won't let me. You know how women are." He cleared his throat.

Mark asked, "Forget what, Hugh?"

"That wagon axle, Mark. You said if Healy didn't pay it you would. He ain't paid it. I dunned him half a dozen times."

Straight was looking at Mark curiously. Mark could feel the unwilling flush that climbed to his face. It gave him away, he thought angrily. Without the flush, he might have passed this off. Now he couldn't.

He fished in his pocket. "How much was it, Hugh?"

"Four and a half, countin' the trip out there. And a quarter for that kid that drove their wagon back to town."

Mark handed him a five-dollar gold piece. Hugh mumbled, "I know it ain't your bill, Mark, but you said . . ."

"Forget it."

Hugh shuffled back to the bar. Straight glanced at Mark quizzically. "What was what all about? You paying Healy's bills for him nowadays?"

Mark said levelly, "I came on Healy's wife and kid a couple of miles outside of town a while back. The wagon was broke down and they didn't have any money. I sent Hugh out to fix them up and told him if Healy didn't pay, I would."

Straight said nothing.

Mark looked at him defiantly. "I'd do the same for any woman that needed help."

Straight said soberly, "Whoa now. I didn't say anything."

"Well, you thought it."

"Maybe. Maybe I did." He looked at Mark quietly. "I've been your friend ever since you came here, Mark. And I'm about to give you some advice. If you don't want it, or if it will make you mad, say so now and I'll keep still."

Mark looked at him. Straight, nearly old enough to be Mark's father, was watching him in a manner both friendly and serious. His brown eyes, with crow's feet of good humor at their corners, were full of concern. Mark muttered, "Go ahead, Phil."

"Well, it's just this. You're ruining yourself. You tried killing yourself with work and when you couldn't do that, you tried liquor. I'm not saying Susan Healy isn't a fine woman. She is. But she isn't yours, Mark. And you can't make her yours."

Mark stood very still. He wanted to hit Phil. He wanted to throw something through the back-bar mirror. After a moment, he said tightly, "So you know. Does the whole damn country know?" There was bitterness in his voice.

"I don't think so. But, Mark, look at it this way. What's in it for you? Susan Healy is a virtuous woman, or I'm no judge. Forget her."

"Forget her?" Mark's words were incredulous. "Don't you think I've tried?"

He stared at Straight for a long minute. Then he said, "Tell the others we'll be in later. I've got to talk to you."

Straight crossed the saloon and went into the back room. In a moment he was back. "All right, Mark. Come on over here in the corner."

Mark followed him and the pair sat down across from each other at the corner table. Straight waited silently for Mark to begin.

Mark frowned, collecting his thoughts. At last he said, "It's a long story, this business between Healy and me. I don't care about the rest of the country knowing it, but I'd like you to."

Straight said nothing.

Mark told him about his experience with the Apaches, about the attack in which his parents were killed. Then he told him about the Ortegas, about Healy and Corbin and Smead. Straight's face showed shock, disbelief.

Mark told him of the trail of vengeance that had led him to Healy, the only one left of the three. He paused, remembering. "He hadn't married Susan, then, but he'd asked her. He was gone when I arrived, but I got to know Susan and fell in love with her."

"Why didn't *you* marry her?"

Mark looked at him. He grinned weakly. "That's a simple enough question, isn't it? Looks like the answer would be simple too. But it isn't. The truth of the matter is, I don't know. I was living on hate in those days. I'd been living on it since I was fourteen.

All I could think was that I had to find Healy. I had to kill him. But before I left to look for him, I figured I owed it to Susan to tell her what he was and what he had done."

"And she didn't believe you."

Mark shook his head.

"I don't blame her. It's an incredible story. It's hard to believe a human being could be that goddam rotten."

Mark said, "Do you know what he's got hanging on his wall out there on the flat?"

Straight shook his head.

"Those Mexican scalps—the ones he took in San Pablo and never collected the bounty on. Susan found them in his things right after she married him. She took them out and buried them. The son of a bitch made her show him where they were and dug them up again. Now he keeps them hangin' on the wall."

Straight asked, "Why'd you come here?"

"I couldn't forget Susan. I figured if I saw her, it would be all over. Only it wasn't. When I saw her, I knew I was more in love with her than ever."

"How about Healy?"

"I thought I'd got over hating him, now I'm not so sure. I want to kill Healy so goddam bad sometimes I can't think of anything else. But I can't kill him. And I can't be the means of his being killed. Do you understand that?"

Straight nodded, beginning to comprehend. "Then that's why you were so damn reluctant this morning?"

Mark nodded. He said, "If you were going to turn Healy over to the law, it might be different. But I know you can't risk that. He'd be tried at the county seat, and over there you couldn't get more than two cowmen out of twelve on the jury. They'd acquit him. And then you'd really be in trouble. Every homesteader on the flats would know it was open season on your cattle."

Straight's face was grim. "I don't like taking the law into our own hands any better than the next man. But we've got no choice. We've got to catch Healy and string him up. We've got to make an example out of him for the rest of the farmers out there on the flats. If we don't, we're finished." He grinned. "One thing, though."

"What's that?"

"I'm going to feel a lot better about it when we do—because of what you've just told me." Straight rose. "Ready to go in?"

Mark nodded, getting to his feet. He followed Straight into the back room, feeling a bleak depression. Nothing was solved. Straight might excuse him from participating in Healy's capture and execution, but he couldn't excuse himself. He was part of this community. Probably he would live out his life here. He had to take his place with the others in solving common problems. And this was the most serious problem any of them would ever face.

The back room of the Stockman's was big and bare. In the center was a pool table. On one wall was a rack of cues, and around the walls were straight-backed chairs.

There were about seven or eight men in the room, mostly gathered in one corner. They looked up as Straight and Mark came in, and their talk stopped.

Mark grabbed a chair and straddled it, leaning his arms on its back. Straight remained standing. He asked, "Decided anything?"

Woolery rumbled, "Only that we've got to get the son of a bitch. Four hundred cattle last year at thirty dollars a head. That's twelve thousand dollars—more than we can afford to lose. It's got to stop."

Straight asked, "Any ideas about how we're going to do it?"

Woolery frowned and shook his head. "The thing that beats us is the system of lookouts they've got. Every homesteader on the flats, whether he's in on the rustling or not, is a lookout for them. That's why they're so damned hard to catch."

Straight said, "Then we've got to put a lookout on Healy."

Woolery nodded, and the others murmured agreement. Straight ignored Mark and glanced at Todd McFee. "How about you taking it tonight. It's a hell of a night, but it's only on the bad nights that they work. Looks like you're dressed warmer than anyone else. You ride over to Healy's place and get as close as you have to so as not to miss him in case he takes a notion to leave. If it's still snowing in the morning, I'll come and relieve you. Otherwise, come on home."

McFee nodded agreement. All the men rose to go. Mark realized that Straight had pointedly excluded him and would probably continue to do so in the future. It was a relief in a way, yet in spite of it, he understood that he could not, forever, exclude himself. The day might come when he would have to choose between his need to stay out of Healy's affairs, and his friends, to whom he had an obligation.

They trooped out through the saloon and onto the walk outside. The others dispersed, leaving Mark and Straight and McFee standing on the walk.

The snow thickened, but it still slanted horizontally along on a driving wind. Most of the stores were dark by now, but lamplight winked from the windows of a few, and from the hotel. A wagon rumbled along the street and stopped before the hotel, vaguely seen through the thick curtain of snow.

Recognition stirred in Mark. "Isn't that Healy's wagon?"

The men beside him stiffened, peering through the gloom. A woman alighted from the wagon, carrying a child, and entered the hotel lobby. In the light from the open door, Mark recognized Susan. He said, "It's Healy, all right. That's his wife going in the hotel."

Straight said, "Let's see where he goes."

They waited, and when the wagon moved on, they followed. Healy tied before Solomon's Saloon and went in.

Straight halted before it and peered through a window. "He's got a bottle and is heading for a table by the wall. Looks like you won't need to watch, Todd. He sure as hell isn't planning anything tonight."

Todd said, "Suits me. It's too cold, anyway. I think I'll go over to Samson's and get in a poker game. Maybe I can take a few bucks out of it before it's time to go home."

Straight said, "I'll go with you. Coming, Mark?"

Mark shook his head. "Nope. I think I'll go home."

He watched McFee and Straight cross the street, leaning against the driving wind. He saw them enter Samson's Store. Then he turned and headed back toward the livery barn, where he'd left his horse.

The livery barn was dark, but he found his horse without difficulty, saddled and led him to the door. He thought of Susan and Abby, who later would be forced to ride all the way back home on the exposed seat of the wagon with a drunken Abe Healy at the reins. He said bitterly, "Damn!" He turned his sheepskin collar up against the wind, and swung to the saddle. Then he took the road toward home.

He had forgotten to wear gloves today, and his hand, holding the reins, quickly turned numb with cold. He alternated it with the other, warming one all the time in his pocket. His mind was busy.

Four hundred cattle! Twelve to fifteen thousand dollars! That was a big take for a single winter. And since Abe Healy was the guiding force behind the rustlers, it followed that he probably had received the lion's share of the take. A third at least. Four or five thousand dollars.

What had he done with it? He couldn't put it in the bank, or it would be evidence against him. He gave his family nothing, spent nothing except for the whisky he drank in Solomon's. And no man could drink up more than a small fraction of that much money in the amount of time Healy was in town. It followed that Healy still had most of the money hidden away somewhere on his place.

But why was he hanging onto it so stingily? Most men would have seen to it that their families were better provided for. Most men would have had some of the good things for themselves.

Certainly Susan would have no knowledge of what Healy was doing, or she would not be so fanatically loyal. Hers was undoubtedly a frantic, pitiful hope that Healy had changed, that he was, at least, honest. Perhaps that explained why he gave her nothing. Perhaps he realized that if he did, he would have to explain where it came from. So he certainly had not hidden it in the house, for there Susan would have found it.

For an instant, hope leaped wildly in Mark's heart. If, somehow, he could prove to Susan that Healy was a rustler . . . Would she leave him then? Would she realize that her loyalty had achieved nothing, would never achieve anything?

Mark didn't know, but it was worth a try.

He unconsciously began to hurry his horse. The snow had begun to pile up now, and there was nearly six inches on the ground. The wind kept it scoured off the road and high spots, made drifts behind obstructions and in the gullies and washouts.

He hesitated at his own turnoff. He didn't like what he was going to do. Snooping and spying went against his grain.

Still, wasn't a man justified in doing what he could to catch a bunch of rustlers? Didn't Mark owe that to Straight and Woolery and the others?

He grinned ruefully, knowing that he was doing this for himself and for himself alone. Then, with that settled, he passed his own turnoff and continued decisively along the road toward Healy's.

Riding, he tried to reconstruct the layout of the place in his mind. There was the house, and a lean-to on one side of the house. There was a brush shelter near the corral. And there was the empty root cellar in the center of the yard.

All would be places where Susan went—all would be places where she might inadvertently discover the money . . . Unless Healy had buried it.

He came to Healy's turnoff and swung left, committed irrevocably now, but knowing also that even if he found the money he could not tell Susan of it. He could not demean himself in her eyes.

It would be useful to him in only one way. It would make him sure, within his own mind, that Healy was the rustler boss.

Chapter 15

H<small>E APPROACHED</small> Healy's place by a circuitous route so that his horse would leave no tracks in the yard. He tied his horse to a plow that lay rusting on the ground a hundred yards behind the corral. Then he approached the place on foot, trying to stay on high ground which the wind would keep scoured clean of tracks.

He realized that there was little chance, in as short a time as he had, that he would discover where Healy has hidden his cache especially if it were buried in the open yard. And yet, Healy might also have buried it either in the lean-to or in the root cellar. In that case Mark's chances of finding it were good.

Nervousness assailed him as he approached the root cellar, but he fought it down. He'd have plenty of warning when Healy returned. Healy would be sodden with drink.

The upper door to the root cellar banged noisily in the wind. Mark propped it open so that its noise would not obscure any of the sounds Healy might make returning, then went down the steps to the lower door, which was fastened with a bent nail stuck through a padlock hasp.

He opened that too, taking time to prop it open with a clod. A musty smell of rotting potatoes struck him immediately. He went in and struck a match.

A rusty lantern hung from a wooden peg driven into

the dirt wall. Mark took it down and shook it tentatively. A sloshing, liquid sound told him it was partly filled.

The match he was holding burned his fingers. He dropped it and fumbled with cold hands for another. He swiped it alight, then raised the lantern chimney and touched the match to its wick.

The lantern gave off a feeble, yellow light that flickered with each gust of wind that struck the exposed part of the cellar. Mark hung it back on its peg.

Now, he turned his attention to the cellar. Its floor was littered with boxes, rotting gunnysacks and trash. In one corner was a pile of rotting potatoes, some of which were sprouting long, pale stems. Carefully, without moving anything, Mark examined the trash that lay scattered so haphazardly on the floor.

Healy would have to get into his cache often, obviously, not only to add to it, but to withdraw the gold he used in Solomon's Saloon. Therefore, there should be some sign. . . .

He knelt to see better. Squinting, he found fingermarks in the dust on one old crate. His blood began to pound.

Carefully, he lifted the crate and set it aside. Beneath it was dry dirt floor, but when Mark touched the dirt with a forefinger, he discovered it was soft and loose.

He went up the stairs and stuck his head out into the wind. He heard nothing. Returning quickly, he began to dig in the soft dirt that had been beneath the crate. He had gone no deeper than a couple of inches when his hand struck part of a canvas sack. Seizing it, he pulled it clear, knowing instantly from its weight that here was the thing he sought.

He untied the drawstring and peered in at the dull gold coins. Then he retied the sack and replaced it in the hole, carefully covering it and smoothing the dirt over it.

He replaced the crate in the exact position it had been before. He blew out the lantern and stepped out, closing the lower door behind him.

Snow had drifted into the open stairwell, but Mark knew any tracks he made would be gone in a matter of minutes. So, he hoped, would the oily smell left in the air by the coal-oil lantern. He stepped out into the blasting wind, and removed the prop from the outer door. Immediately it began to bang again in the wind.

Heading across the yard toward the corral, behind which he had tied his horse, Mark was startled by a shout behind him. He halted immediately, listening. The shout had come from some distance away.

Over the howl of the wind, he heard the clank of chain tugs and the rattle of harness rings. He heard the squeak of wagon wheels in the snow.

He sprinted for his horse, and reaching him, stopped to listen again. Though he could not see Healy's wagon, he could hear it well. Surprisingly, it stopped at the house, probably to let Susan and Abby off, though Mark doubted if Healy was usually this considerate. Then it continued, to stop again beside the corral.

Mark stood still, ready to muffle the nostrils of his horse should the animal scent Healy's team and try to nicker. He heard the rattle of harness as Healy removed it, and the louder jangle as he flung it, one set at a time, over the corral fence. Then he heard the squeak of the corral gate.

So far his horse had not smelled the team. Taking a chance that he wouldn't now, Mark left him and walked through the shroud of snow toward Healy's yard. He saw Healy's bulk leave the corral and stride across to the house, in which a lamp now flickered feebly. The door opened, releasing the sound of Abby's crying.

Poor little kid, thought Mark. She was probably half frozen, and the warmth of the house made her hands and feet hurt.

Why he stayed after that, he couldn't have said. Just thinking of Susan inside with Healy made anger boil in his mind. But he waited, knowing he wouldn't leave until the lamp went out. Straight and the others had thought Healy was in town to go on a drunk, something he usually did when he came to town. But they'd been mistaken. There had been no hint of unsteadiness in Healy's walk as he went across the yard. His steps had been sure and straight.

The lamp went out inside the house and Mark turned toward his horse.

But he stopped as he heard the door again, and

whirled around. He saw Healy come, still fully dressed, from the door. He watched Healy cross the yard to the corral. Excitement stirred in Mark. He realized that his hands were trembling.

A scarf was tied over Healy's head under his hat. Obviously he wore heavy gloves, for his hands were clumsy as he bridled a horse. He led the horse out, and kicked around in the snow beside the corral gate until he found his saddle.

He saddled quickly and mounted. Then he rode out of the yard into the blinding snowstorm.

Immediately Mark swung into his own saddle. Following only by sound and not by sight, he trailed Healy out of the yard. Healy headed east.

As he rode, Mark's mind seethed with uncertainty. This was the chance Straight would have given an arm for, but Mark didn't know whether he wanted to take it or not.

Damn it, why had they let Healy throw them off so easily? Healy had come to town deliberately, for that purpose. He'd set up a pattern, on his previous visits to Solomon's, of getting drunk, of staying several hours. And he'd come into town tonight to make them think just what they'd thought.

Todd McFee should have been the one to catch Healy—not Mark. Now, he didn't know what to do. Following Healy would inevitably involve him in Healy's capture and subsequent death. Discovering how it was done, Susan must despise him for it. She would think he had lacked the courage to kill Healy openly and so had chosen this devious way, letting others do his killing for him.

Mark cursed bitterly, his ears still tuned to the faint sounds of Healy traveling before him. How would he ever explain his presence here tonight to Susan? How would he ever convince her that he had not been stalking Healy for personal reasons?

And yet, how could he abandon this trail, when he knew how much catching Healy meant to his friends? He thought of Straight, whose young wife and kids would have to do without for a whole year because of the cattle Healy had stolen. He thought of Joe Weems, who might lose his ranch because of the rustling.

He shook his head angrily. Then, with his face strained and cold, he put aside his doubts and concentrated on following Healy through the night. He had no choice—had never had a choice. There was only one course for him.

He was forced to lift his horse to a trot, but soon he discovered that he could follow Healy by sight if he did not fall too far behind. The snow, over six inches deep, left a plain trail where Healy's horse had gone, visible because it was darker than the surrounding blanket of stark white. But he couldn't fall too far behind, or the wind would cover the trail. Nor could he get too close, or Healy, hearing some slight sound on his backtrail, might pause and ambush him.

The trail went on endlessly, heading straight east. Half an hour passed. But at last, Mark heard a shout before him, and drew his horse to an immediate halt.

Sitting there, he could dimly see the dark bulk of a house in the distance ahead. A square of light showed as a door opened, and Mark heard the muffled sound of voices. Then the door closed again.

Mark waited. Healy was gathering his crew. That was obvious. Probably no one knew when Healy would make a raid—no one but Healy himself. Working this way, there was little chance of their being discovered. And perhaps it explained why they had been so successful thus far.

Again the square of light showed through the snow, and again Mark heard the muffled voices. Then the door closed, and after a few moments Mark moved on, slowly and carefully, until he struck the trail he sought, now a trail of two horses.

His senses sharpened with the feel of danger. An ambush now would mean certain death for Mark. His hands were stiff with cold. His gun was buried under his heavy, soggy sheepskin—it would take him a week to get it out.

He followed for another fifteen minutes, then halted a second time while Healy entered another house. After that he found he was following the tracks of four horses instead of two.

The trail swung south, and continued in that direction for more than an hour before it swung again, this time toward the west. This would be Phil Straight's place. West of it lay Woolery's MW outfit, and beyond that, Joe Weems's place.

Mark heard the bawl of cattle ahead, and slowed.

Moving forward cautiously, he found where Healy and his companions had picked up several head of cattle in the lee of a bluff. And now the trail was very plain, containing the tracks of half a dozen cattle in addition to those of the rustlers' four horses.

These cattle were probably Straight's. But, moving across the range, they'd probably pick up some of Woolery's steers and a few from Weems's place. Beyond that lay the hogback, which guarded the approaches to the mountains.

Mark began to wonder just what he expected to accomplish by following the rustlers. If he trailed them long enough to learn exactly where they were going, it would be too late to return to Arriola for help. Yet he knew, too, that jumping four men was a suicidal risk that was doomed to failure.

He decided that the best he could do was learn something of their plans so that he could ride for help and later intercept them. Thinking this way, he lifted his horse to a running walk, an almost silent gait, and after ten minutes raised the dim shapes of men and cattle.

He did not underestimate the danger of getting in so close. If he could hear their talk, they could also hear him. His horse, scenting theirs, might whinny and give him away. Yet in his favor was the fact that they felt safe, and alone. Also in his favor was the cover of snow on the ground, which would deaden the sounds of his horse's hoofs.

He heard their sour, grumpy voices complaining of

the cold, of the hour, of the driving snow. He heard Abe Healy snarl, "Quit your goddam bellyachin'. You figger it's easier to make a living farming?"

For a while there was silence, broken only by an occasional curse. Tension was high in Mark, for he was far too close. And yet, he knew of no other way to accomplish his purpose. He had to know where they were going before he dared leave them and ride to town.

Another hour passed. Mark's body was chilled clear through. His hands were numb. Snow, driving against his right side, had soaked his face, his collar, his pants legs, for he wore no chaps.

Some more grumbling, and then at last a young voice asked, "Which way we takin' these, Mr. Healy? We goin' to put 'em clear through to the mines tonight?"

And Abe Healy's deep, surly voice came again, "Hell, no. We've got to have light to butcher."

Again there was silence. Mark rode numbly, his ears straining. At last Healy spoke again. "This goddam storm is worse than I figured. If it keeps on getting worse, we won't even get to the mines tomorrow. We'll have to lay over the other side of the hogback."

Mark drew back on his reins instantly. His horse stopped, and ahead all sounds died as the rustlers moved away. Mark drew his sheepskin closer around his neck. He held his numbed hands over his ears a moment to try and warm them.

He guessed he had as much information as he'd ever get. He knew how lucky he was to have got this much. He knew their destination and he knew where they'd lay over if the storm got worse, which it seemed to be doing.

He estimated that right now he was almost due south of Arriola, and judged that the rustlers were heading almost due west. Therefore, he took a bearing on the direction the rustlers had gone, then turned at right angles toward the north.

He faced almost directly into the wind now, and knew he could guide himself on the wind. Pray God it didn't shift.

He was not too familiar with Woolery's range, but he had covered most of it on roundup, and so knew a few of the landmarks. Riding blind through the driving snow, occasionally he would glimpse one, and alter his course accordingly.

Several hours had passed since he'd left town. Straight and Woolery might have left. If they had, there was nothing he could do. If he took time to ride to their separate ranches for them, the rustlers would probably get away.

He understood that he could still back out of this. He could still swing east and go on home. Or he could ride to Healy's shack and tell Susan what Healy was doing. His failure to put the other cowmen on Healy would set up an obligation that Susan would feel deeply.

Mark scowled suddenly, wishing he could be as

unscrupulous as some men could. But he did not turn toward Healy's place. Instead he continued on toward town.

When the chips were down, a man could only do what his conscience let him do. Mark's wouldn't let him buy Susan with Healy's safety.

Chapter 16

IT WAS ALMOST ELEVEN when Mark raised the town's dim lights ahead. He hurried his horse, feeling as though his body was chilled clear through. He could not recall ever having been quite so cold. His hand, holding the reins, was as stiff as if it were frozen.

He entered Main Street, noting that the Stockman's was still open, but that Solomon's was closed. Before the Stockman's, three horses stood in miserable dejection.

Mark dismounted, nearly falling as his numbed feet touched the snowy ground. He recovered, and tried to loop his reins around the rail. After a couple of clumsy failures, he finally succeeded and stumbled into the smoky warmth of the saloon.

Inside, he brushed ineffectually at the snow that covered him. His face was grim as he stepped across to the stove.

Straight came from the bar at once, his face solemn with concern. "Man, what happened to you? You look half froze." Straight had his coat buttoned up and a muffler tied over his head and under his chin to protect his ears. Another five minutes, and Mark would have missed him entirely.

Mark rubbed his hands, frowning at the pain. His feet felt like stumps. He said, "I've got what we want. Where's Woolery and McFee? Still playing poker?"

"What do you mean, you've got what we want? I thought you went home."

Mark shook his head impatiently. "I went out to Healy's to snoop around. I was there when he came home. Hell, he just came to town to throw you off. Soon's you quit watching him, he went on home."

"You mean he's making a raid?"

Mark nodded. "He left, soon's he got home, rode east and picked up three more men. Then he moved south onto your range and picked up a small bunch of your stuff. He swung west after that toward the mountains. When I left him, on Woolery's range, he had twelve or fifteen head."

Excitement made Straight's eyes bright. He chortled, "And you know where they're headed?"

Mark nodded. "The mining camp. But I think they'll hole up for a while the other side of the hogback. The storm's too thick and getting worse. It's a chance I had to take. I couldn't take them on alone."

His hands were burning now, alive with pain. So were his feet. "Let me stand here a minute. We'll either catch them or we won't, but I can't ride out again until I'm warm."

His coat began to steam. A drowsiness came over him. Straight went to the bar, got a tumbler half full of whisky and brought it to him. Mark drank it grate-fully, reveling in the warmth of it coursing down his throat and spreading through his belly.

The minutes passed, and gradually the chill left him and he began to feel comfortable again. He worked his hands tentatively.

At last he said, "All right. Let's go get Woolery and McFee. I can pick up a muffler and a pair of gloves while we're there."

They went out into the savagely driving snow. Straight shivered. "Hell of a night for riding." He gripped Mark's shoulder as they crossed the street. "Mark, damn it, don't be so close-mouthed. What'd you find out at Healy's? What were you lookin' for?"

"I'll tell you later." The wind snatched the words from Mark's mouth and flung them away.

Samson's Store was dark, save for a dim light that shone through the open door of the back room. Straight pounded heavily on the front door. It rattled under his blows. After a long interval, Mark heard Samson's stomping steps and his sour-voiced, irri-table, "Who the hell's that?"

Straight shouted, "It's Straight and Atkins! Let us in! We got to talk to Mel!"

Mark heard the sounds of a padlock being with-drawn from the hasp. Then the door swung open pon-derously. Mark went in and Straight followed. He went down the long aisle, followed by Straight and a grumbling Samson.

The back room was filled with smoke. Woolery sat

at a poker table with McFee and his own hired man, Slim Hankins. He boomed, "Want to try your luck, Mark?"

Mark shook his head. Straight spoke excitedly behind him. "Mark's got the goods on 'em, Mel. Get your coat and let's get after 'em!"

"You mean Healy?"

Mark nodded. "He's got three men and a bunch of cattle. He's on your range right now, heading for the mountains."

"How the hell we goin' to find 'em in this?"

"Mark figures they'll hole up on the other side of the hogback, to wait for daylight."

Samson went to the table and picked up his cards. He said sourly, "Damn you, Mel, you can't quit now. You've got all the money."

Woolery laughed. "Get even some other time." He got up and flung his cards on the table. He scooped his money up and stuffed it into his pocket. Hankins and McFee followed suit.

Mark said, "Samson, I need gloves and a muffler. And overshoes if you've got 'em."

Samson carried the lamp up front. Mark picked out a muffler and riffled through a pile of gloves, looking for his size. Samson had brought out a pair of canvas and rubber overshoes made to fit a high-heeled boot. Mark took off his spurs and put them on. He stuffed the spurs into the pocket of his sheep-skin.

The others waited impatiently, oddly silent, while

he tied the muffler over his head and crammed his hat over it. He said, "All right, let's go."

Samson opened the door for them. "What're you goin' to do to them if you catch them?" he asked.

Straight's voice had a nervous edge to it. "What do you think, Samson? This bunch got nearly four hundred head from us last year."

The five went out through the door and into the blasting wind. Samson locked the door behind them.

Even the Stockman's Saloon was closed now. Woolery swung ponderously to his horse, tied before Samson's Store. McFee and Hankins were quick to follow. Mark and Straight walked across the street and got their horses from in front of the Stockman's.

Straight and Mark led out. The five were a silent bunch, knowing a good many hard, cold miles lay ahead, knowing too that death waited at the end of the trail. Death for Healy and his rustlers; death, perhaps, for one or more of the five cowmen.

Once, Todd McFee grumbled, "Why the hell couldn't they have picked a decent night? Brrrr!" But there was no real complaint in his voice.

Angling southwest, they crossed the empty miles of bleak, cold range. There was no talk, only grim, unrelenting purpose.

A certain hopelessness possessed Mark, for he had passed the point of no return. He was committed now, committed to join the others in whatever they did to Healy and his men.

Susan would hear the details; everyone in the

196

country would. She would hear that Mark had been skulking around Healy's house, looking for Healy's gold. She would hear that was the way he had caught Healy. She would know it was Mark who followed her husband, and rode to town for help, then helped catch and hang Healy and those who were with him.

They swung due west now, and after two more hours sighted the dim bulk of the hogback before them. Straight shouted, "Where do you reckon we ought to look first, Mark?"

Mark thought a moment. Then he yelled back, "They'd want shelter. Don't you suppose they'd pick those red sandstone rocks to hole up in?"

Straight nodded. There was a cut in the hogback through which Arriola Creek tumbled and they rode into it cautiously, studying the ground as they rode. In one sheltered spot, they found tracks, not only of cattle, but of horses too. There was also a mound of dung still steaming in the cold air.

Straight reined up, pointing. He said, "Quiet, now. They ain't over fifteen or twenty minutes ahead of us."

Mark began to wonder what he would do when they jumped the rustlers. Perhaps it would be easier for all concerned if he lined his sights on Healy and shot the man. It would save Susan the knowledge that her husband had been hanged.

No one would know whose bullet had killed Healy. Scowling, Mark shook his head. Maybe they wouldn't, but *he* would.

The snow had thinned in the past half hour. Now the moon peeped through the thinning clouds. That meant Healy would not lay over here until morning as planned. He'd drive straight through. But it no longer mattered. Mark and the others had a trail to follow again.

They turned right upon leaving the gorge and began to rise through the arroyo-cut valley. Ahead loomed the dim and grotesque shapes of the red sandstone rocks. Some of them were several hundred feet high.

Mark kept his glance on the ground, following the tracks which had not drifted in so badly in this sheltered valley as they had out on the plain. The tracks were fresh—very fresh.

Suddenly, the bawl of a steer came eerily out of the drifting gloom ahead, magnified many times by the looming rock behind it, echoing back from other rock faces beyond. A murmur of indistinct voices followed.

Straight said shortly, "All right. Spread out. Don't let a damned one get away. If they try, shoot to kill."

Straight fell away to the left with Todd McFee. Woolery took Slim Hankins off to the right, which left Mark alone in the middle.

He slipped off his right glove, flexing his hand. He took his Colt's .44 out from under his sheepskin and held it loosely in his hand. He picked his way through a brush pocket as silently as he could, and when he rode clear on the other side, saw them there, unexpectedly, before him.

They had built a small fire, and were clustered around it, hunkering on the ground, their hands spread toward the fire. Behind them the cattle bunched, unmoving and dispirited.

Abe Healy squatted, big and black-bearded, on the other side of the fire from Mark. He was scowling. His eyes, catching the light of the fire, appeared red. Unaware of Mark sitting there half concealed by brush, he spat a stream of tobacco juice into the fire. The hiss of it was plainly audible to Mark.

Standing abruptly, Healy grunted, "All right. Kick snow on the fire and let's go."

From somewhere off to Mark's left a voice spoke, Straight's voice. "Wait a minute, boys. Don't move!"

Healy halted as though frozen. Then he stooped to snatch at his rifle leaning against a nearby rock. Straight's voice cut like a whip. "Touch it, you son of a bitch, and you're dead!"

Healy straightened, a slump of resignation in his shoulders. Not so the others. A young voice shouted hysterically, "They'll hang us! I'll . . ."

The form of a grown boy detached itself from the group at the fire. Half running, half crawling, he reached Healy's rifle and snatched it up. Whirling, he fired. Flame spat from its muzzle.

Flat and wicked came the answering two shots from behind the brush screen to Mark's left. The boy let go of the gun and it fell into the snow beside the fire.

Mark saw that there was pale fuzz on the boy's face—a face that was sick with fear. The boy fumbled at the buttons of his sheepskin, but before he got it open, he folded silently and tiredly to the ground.

An older man knelt over him and tore open the coat, his shoulders shaking visibly. He ripped back the boy's shirt. Then he laid his whiskered face against the boy's chest.

Mark rode out of the brush. He could see the shadowy forms of the others coming up from right and left. Healy stood scowling. Another man stood beside him, terrified, his face working silently.

The man on the ground rose from the dead boy's side. He had the rifle in his hands. Holding the gun at hip level, he swung the muzzle in a tight arc toward Straight. His face was bloodless, his eyes tortured. Tears streamed across his weathered, whiskered cheeks.

Mark could have shot him. But, shocked by the suddenness and violence of the boy's death, he couldn't move.

A shot racketed from Mark's right, where Woolery and Hankins were, echoed almost instantly by the rifle held by the man at the fire. Then the man was falling, falling across the limp body of his son.

The cattle spooked away into the brush, frightened out of their lethargy by the noise.

Straight issued a crisp command. "Slim, you and Todd go read the brands on them cattle. Not that it's necessary, but I don't want anything in doubt." He turned to Healy. "We been after you for a long time and this is the end of the track. Want to write your wife a letter?"

Healy shook his head. Straight looked at the other man. "How about you?"

The man nodded and Straight rode up and gave him a scrap of paper and the stub of a pencil. The man sat down and tried to write on his knee, but his hands were shaking so badly that he gave it up and flung both paper and pencil into the fire.

Woolery had taken down his rope and was now fashioning a hangman's noose. Healy did not seem to see Straight or Woolery at all. He was looking at Mark. "You're the one, ain't you? I didn't know until tonight. Hugh Neff said you paid my bill with him."

Mark was silent.

Healy said, "Skulkin' around behind my back! You dirty bastard!"

Mark clenched his teeth. His face was white. He said, "You know me, Healy. My name's Mark Atkins. Only you knew me as Marcos Ortega."

Healy's face wore a blank look of puzzlement, and an odd uneasiness. It was as though he remembered the name from some remote part of his own past.

Mark said, "San Pablo, you murdering bastard!"

Healy's face turned gray.

Mark said, "Except for Susan, you'd have been dead long before this." He stared bleakly at Healy. And suddenly he knew what he had to do.

He swung off his horse. He unbuttoned his coat and shrugged it off. He put the .44 in one of the side pockets of the coat and hung it on his saddlehorn. Then he said with flat hostility, "You've used your fists on your wife. Try them now on someone who can fight back."

Abe Healy showed momentary surprise. Then, in his narrowed eyes shone a sly kind of hope. He came forward, shoulders hunched, fists cocked.

Straight put his horse between them like a wall. He said harshly, "Mark, we're hanging him. It ain't decent to beat him first."

Mark looked up. His eyes were cold. "We're not hanging him. Get out of my way."

For an instant their glances locked. Then, mumbling something, Straight nudged his horse forward.

Mark knew a brief moment's fear. If he lost . . . he'd lose everything. Healy would be hanged because Mark would be in no condition to prevent it. And Susan would hate him forever because he had tried to beat Healy with his fists as a prelude to the hanging. She would never understand or believe what he was trying to do.

Chapter 17

A BE HEALY came in with a rush. He outweighed Mark by a full thirty pounds, and he was hard. His chest was like a bellows. Fear would make him as savage as a cornered animal.

But Mark had hate that crawled in his mind like a thing alive. He had the memory of Jaime and Rosa María Ortega, of the dry scalps hanging on Healy's wall, of the pale face of Susan.

Healy's left fist caught Mark high on the forehead like the blow of a sledge. Healy's right caught him full in the mouth, smashing his lips against his teeth. Healy's knee, raising smoothly and with no waste motion, came up toward Mark's groin.

Mark twisted, avoiding its crippling effect, taking it on his thigh instead. Healy was too close for the use of fists, so Mark brought his right elbow slashing around to catch Healy full in the throat.

The man gagged, and the pair went down into the snow.

Sliding, scrambling, Mark clawed his way clear. Healy, too, was fighting his way to his feet, panting, gagging, mouthing obscenities about the things he thought Mark and Susan had done behind his back.

Rage leaped in Mark like a white-hot flame. His fist smashed out, with every bit of his weight behind it. It connected with Healy's mouth, instantly silencing it. Mark's left, following the right, sank into Healy's middle, driving a grunt of pain from him.

Again the right and again the left, cutting Healy's cheek, his craggy brow. Mark didn't even feel Healy's blows. He absorbed them, and flung them aside, and drove on forward.

His brain was afire, and there was in him a killing fury, a single-minded need to destroy. Again and again his fists smashed into Healy's mouth, as though he could make the man incapable of talk, incapable of contaminating Susan with his words. He knew he was cutting his knuckles to the bone on Healy's teeth, but he didn't care. All he cared about was silencing the man before him.

He was carrying the fight, and forcing Healy back. Blood from Healy's mouth and his own blood mingled on his fists, making them slick and slippery. And Healy, panting heavily, had stopped talking at last, saving his breath for the fight he knew he well might lose.

Healy retreated slowly, the fire at his back. His foot touched a rock, and swiftly he stooped to seize it.

Mark rushed—and instantly understood that Healy had not intended to seize the rock, but stooped only as a ruse. He was caught on Healy's broad, powerful back as the man rose. He felt Healy's grip on his thighs for the briefest instant, and then was flying in mid-air.

He landed squarely in the fire, sending up a cloud of smoke and sparks that completely enveloped him. The hot breath of the fire seared his lungs. His numbed and bleeding hands plunged into it.

A scream of pain escaped his lips. He rolled frantically, saved only by the fact that his clothes were wet. But scarcely had he rolled clear when Healy leaped, his heavy boots smashing into Mark's middle with all his weight behind him.

A gust of air was expelled from Mark's lungs. His belly burned with excruciating pain. But his hatred and fury burned brighter still; his tortured hands seized one of Healy's boots and he rolled again.

Healy fell ponderously, now touching the scattered

fire. Then Mark was clawing up his body, the way a cat will climb a tree. Straddling Healy, he seized the man's beard. With it savagely caught in both his hands, he raised Healy's head and slammed it ferociously back against the ground, again and again, while Healy's arms and hands beat at his face, his chest, trying to force him away.

Nausea, born of pain, soared through Mark. And suddenly he wanted to laugh—this was really illogical. Healy was fighting as though for his life, but victory could only bring him the choking pressure of the hangman's noose and a broken neck.

Healy arched his body like that of a bucking horse. Mark was flung clear, and his hands, torn loose from Healy's beard, pulled off some of the beard, and skin came too. Healy screeched like a wounded cat. Then he was up, kicking viciously at Mark's rolling body, stomping it.

A kick on his shoulder sent him rolling again. He tried to rise, and knew in that instant that it was almost over. Healy's advantage in weight had beaten him after all.

But he thought of San Pablo and he thought of Susan. He looked into the animal mask that was Healy's face, and hatred brought the strength to his body that he had to have. He rose, staggering, and stood spread-legged, glaring like a wounded wolf, snarling . . .

Healy stepped in for the kill, sure at last. He swung, and missed because Mark staggered. They closed and

Mark brought up a knee into Healy's groin.

Abe released him and doubled. Mark stared at him dumbly, surprised that Healy looked quite as sick as he himself felt.

Then he swung his right, putting into it every bit of his remaining strength. He started the blow behind him, and swung it wide, twisting with shoulders and hips, throwing his fist the way a man throws a ball. He knew if it missed he was done. He'd fall, and stay down because he had not the strength to rise again.

But the blow did not miss. With a crack like that of lightning striking a giant pine, it slammed into the side of Healy's jaw.

The jawbone gave with a second crack, like an echo of the first. Healy staggered back, out, but still on his feet. Quietly, then, he folded face forward into the snow, his jaw hanging open and oddly twisted . . .

It took Mark's stunned mind an instant to comprehend that he had won. He swung his reddened eyes to Straight, still on horseback, and then to Woolery's reddened, fascinated face. Then he staggered toward his own horse, knowing he had to reach him before his friends recovered.

Smelling blood, the animal spooked, but Mark stepped on a trailing rein, then stooped to pick it up. He almost fell, dizziness fuzzing his sense of balance.

Straightening, he quieted the horse with a mumbled curse. He fumbled for his coat.

But he didn't put it on. He got the .44 from the side pocket and turned, thumbing back the hammer. He put the muzzle unsteadily on Straight. "You're not hanging anyone," he panted.

Phil didn't say anything for a full minute. Then he asked softly, "What about the other one?"

Mark sat down in the snow heavily. Exhaustion nearly claimed him. But the muzzle of the .44 stayed on Straight. "To hell with him," Mark said.

He felt as though he'd never get enough of this cold, sweet air into his lungs. He breathed with great, long, sucking gasps. He stared emptily at Straight and Woolery as they hustled the struggling rustler away into a grove of trees.

Abe Healy sat up. His jaw hung loose and his eyes were flat with pain. Mark struggled to his feet. He said, "Get your horse and follow me."

Healy got up with difficulty. He walked to a scrub oak where his horse was tied. The light of the fire had faded now, but the moon overhead and the line of dawn in the eastern sky had replaced it with an eerie, cold glow. Mark walked in the direction Straight and Woolery had gone until he saw the last of the rustlers, swinging in the air beneath the gnarled branch of a tree. He said, "Take a good look, you son of a bitch! If you ever come within a hundred miles of Arriola again, you'll look just like him. Now get on your horse and hightail it out of here before I change my mind."

He waited for Healy to mount, while Straight and Woolery stood watching him. He listened to the diminishing drum of hoofs.

Exhaustion and relief nearly claimed him. He knew he had been a fool. Healy was an animal, and should never have gone free.

He turned to Straight. "There's around five thousand in gold in Healy's cellar. I know damned well his wife wouldn't touch it. I hope she won't need it. Maybe it will repay you and the others for part of what you've lost."

He shrugged into his coat painfully. He mounted with difficulty. Neither Straight nor Woolery said anything, nor did they look again at the swinging corpse. Mark rode out alone, heading at last for home.

Chapter 18

THE MILES were long, and cold, and weariness was a weight that clouded Mark's thoughts. Pain ran the length of his body.

The sun came up and hung like a cold and brassy ball above the sterile whiteness of the world. At seven-thirty he rode into his home yard.

He turned his horse into the barn and clawed some hay out of the loft for him. Then he went to the house and stuck his head under the shocking, icy stream that came from the faucet. Filling the dipper to the brim, he took a long, cold drink.

He found a towel and dried himself. Peering into a mirror, he mopped at the blood that had caked on his face. After that, with every muscle screaming, he changed his clothes. Lastly he put tallow on his hands and awkwardly bandaged them with strips torn from a clean flour sack.

He looked longingly at the bed, then went out to stand uncertainly on the stoop. He was beginning to realize what he had done. Divorce was an uncertain and long, drawn-out procedure, taking years sometimes, yet now, with Healy alive, it was the only way Susan could ever be free.

He had cut her loose from the tenuous support Abe gave her and sent him away so that now Susan and Abby were alone. He knew he would offer financial assistance to Susan while she was getting her divorce, but he knew, too, that she would refuse it. He began to wonder, now, if when the divorce was granted, she would still want him.

He shrugged dispiritedly and walked across the yard to the barn. He saddled a fresh horse with difficulty and mounted stiffly. He rode along the road south out of his meadow.

Earlier, the thing he had done had seemed logical, but now it did not seem so at all.

Once he hesitated and almost turned back. But then he thought of Susan, knowing he should be the one to tell her. Afterward, he doggedly kept to his course.

At the main road he halted, seeing two horsemen coming toward him from town. He waited, curious. After a few moments he recognized them as Straight and Woolery.

They rode up to him. Straight said, with some sheepishness, "We got to thinking about that gold you said Healy had. We figured he might come back for it. You went too damn easy on that bastard, Mark, and he shouldn't have the gold. It rightly belongs to us and to Joe Weems. It'll save Joe's place."

Mark shrugged. "All right. Come on, I'll show you where it is."

They went on silently, turning to the left at Healy's place. After a few more minutes they topped the long rise that hid Healy's house and the vast flat behind it, and could see down into his yard.

Two horses stood saddled beside the house. Healy, unmistakable even at this distance, sat ponderously on one of them holding his jaw and apparently arguing with Susan who stood near by. Abby stood alone, small and frightened, her glance switching back and forth from one to the other.

Straight cursed bitterly. "Damn him, this time he's pushed his luck too far!" He dug spurs into his horse and galloped down the slope, with Woolery and Mark pounding along close behind.

Abe whirled at the sound of hoofs. Mark was closer now, and could see that his face was ugly with rage and with pain from the broken jaw. Healy's hand shot to the revolver at his hip.

Straight raised his rifle without slackening speed. Mark bellowed, "Put that damn gun up! You might hit . . ." His words were almost lost in the roar of Healy's revolver.

But Healy had heard. And apparently the possibilities behind Mark's words sank into his mind.

210

Thrusting the revolver into his belt, he gigged his horse aside, leaned down and picked up the screaming child by one arm. He clutched her body against him with the hand that held the reins. With the other, he again drew the revolver from his belt.

Straight yanked his plunging horse to a halt. He faced Healy's menacing gun uncertainly. Mark and Woolery drew up, sliding, beside him.

There was an instant, then, when all was still. Mark looked at Susan and felt something sick in his heart. One of her eyes was bruised and swelling. There was blood at the corner of her pretty mouth.

She looked up dispiritedly at Mark. When she spoke, her voice was discouraged and disillusioned. "He hadn't changed. He had a sack of gold hidden in the cellar. He's been stealing cattle ever since he came here."

Mark tried to smile at her. "Did you really think he could change?"

She said wearily, "I hoped he could."

Straight spoke sharply. "Healy, put that kid down! You're finished. Mark kept you from hanging, but God Almighty can't keep you from me now!"

Healy's teeth were clenched against the awful pain of his broken jaw. His eyes were hot, wild, dangerous. He was as deadly, as unpredictable, right now as a tormented rattler, and likely to strike in any direction.

Mark realized that Healy was fighting himself, fighting against his almost insane desire to kill Mark, whom he blamed for all his troubles. But he seemed to know that if he did, not even Abby could save his life.

Through clenched teeth, he spoke to his wife harshly. "Susan, get up on that goddam horse!"

He switched his glance to Mark. His speech was thick and blurred by pain and by ungovernable fury. "We're leaving this damned country, all three of us. I'll have Abby on my saddle all day. I'll have her beside me all night. Don't try to follow or I'll kill her and Susan both."

All the things Mark wanted to say to Susan he put into his glance. She smiled up at him with tears in her eyes as though she understood. Then she prepared to mount her horse.

Healy was watching Mark balefully and hungrily, and so did not see the thing Susan did next. Snatching her shawl from her head, she flung it at the head of her husband's horse.

Unused to women and to women's garb, the horse did what Susan had known he would. He shied violently and reared. Healy, with an entirely instinctive gesture, released Abby and grabbed for the saddle-horn. As the child fell, the horse shied away from her and reared again. Susan darted in under his hoofs and snatched Abby from the ground. The child's face was white, her eyes flat with utter terror. She began to scream.

Healy's jaw muscles had relaxed enough to let his mouth fall open. He groaned sharply with pain. With one hand, the one that held the reins, he closed his jaw. With the other, the one that held the gun, he slammed the horse savagely between the ears.

The animal dropped to all four feet and stood there, stunned. Healy, wholly out of control now, raised his gun and centered its muzzle on Mark. He thumbed back the hammer.

Mark's gun was under his coat. His hands were bandaged and hurt. He was helpless. But he knew, suddenly, that even if he were not, he could not have killed Healy. He had gone to too much trouble to spare the man. If Healy were ever killed, someone else would have to do it. He stared at the black bore of Healy's gun and waited for the shock of the heavy bullet.

But Healy never fired. Straight's rifle spat wickedly. Abe was driven sideways, and his gun spun out of his hand. It discharged as it hit the ground, and the bullet sang harmlessly off into space.

Susan stared dumbly for a moment at Abe, awkwardly sprawled on the ground at her feet. Then, quickly covering Abby's face with a trembling hand, she picked up the child and ran for the house. She slammed the door hard behind her.

Straight swung down. He walked to Healy warily and toed the man roughly with his boot. Healy rolled limply. His vacant, dead eyes stared at the sky. Straight said, "Mel, gimme a hand."

Mel dismounted. Between them they hoisted Healy to his horse. Mel tied him down. Straight looked at

Mark as he mounted, holding the reins of the horse on which Healy was tied. "So long, Mark."

Mark's grin was like a grimace. He watched them ride away and disappear over the knoll that hid the road to town.

Then he turned and knocked softly on the door.

Susan's face was gray with shock as she answered it. Mark said soberly, "You have to know this. I led them to him. I argued it out with myself and I . . . ."

"You did what you had to do, Mark. I know how hard it was." Her expression was soft and pitying, and her eyes were shy.

His heart jumped. "You don't blame me, then?"

"How could I blame you? You were right about Abe. You were always right. He was vicious. There in the yard he would have killed both Abby and me as quickly as he would have killed you." She tried to smile, but it was a tremulous failure.

Mark opened his mouth to speak, but Susan stopped him, touching his mouth with a gentle hand. "Be quiet about it, Mark. It's over. Come in and have some breakfast."

Suddenly, then, she was in his arms, warm and soft, an eager girl on the verge of tears and hysteria. Mark held her close, close enough to feel her heart beating against his own.

Her body trembled, and at last she began to weep, wildly and hysterically. He held her away and kissed her face, so warm and soft, so wet with tears.

Abby came shyly across the room and looked up

timidly at him. He patted the child's smooth head.

He sighed—a soft, contented sigh. The long trail was behind him, and this was the promise that had been at its end. This was the promise, fulfilled at last.

Center Point Publishing
600 Brooks Road ● PO Box 1
Thorndike ME 04986-0001 USA

(207) 568-3717

US & Canada:
1 800 929-9108
www.centerpointlargeprint.com